U0032615

漢字

365

每日
一字

A Character a Day
Mastering Basic Vocabulary for
Everyday Life

目次
Table of Contents

前言
Preface

Many Chinese learners have problems building up their vocabulary of Chinese characters, but if we did it by learning one character a day, maybe it would be much easier.

This simple, illustrated book is designed to help you learn one Chinese character a day and provides information on character evolution, stroke order, explanations, related terms, and example sentences. By studying one character and a minimum of two supplementary terms each day, you can learn some 1000 words in just one year.

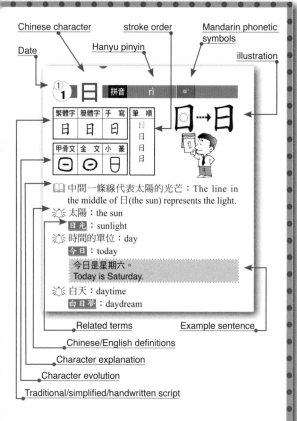

The characters are written in traditional, simplified, and handwritten script and come with illustrations, pinyin, Mandarin phonetic symbols, English explanations, related terms, and example sentences.

An index based on the pinyin spelling of the characters makes it easier to look up characters in the book.

1 月
January

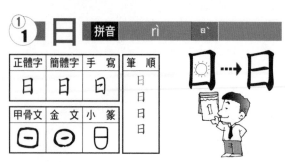

正體字	簡體字	手 寫	筆 順
日	日	日	日 日 日 日

甲骨文	金 文	小 篆
⊖	⊖	(日)

拼音　rì

📖 中間一條線代表太陽的光芒：The line in the middle of 日(the sun) represents the light.

☀ 太陽：the sun

　　日光：sunlight

☀ 時間的單位：day

　　今日：today

　　今日是星期六。
　　Today is Saturday.

☀ 白天：daytime

　　白日夢：daydream

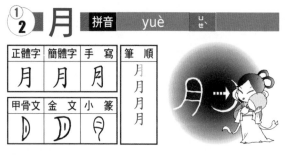

正體字	簡體字	手 寫	筆 順
月	月	月	月 月 月 月

甲骨文	金 文	小 篆
D	D	(月)

拼音　yuè

📖 像弦月的形狀：月 takes the shape of a crescent moon.

　　月亮：the moon

　　滿月：the full moon

　　今晚的月色明亮。
　　We have a bright moon tonight.

☀ 時間的單位：month

　　一個月：one month

　　月刊：monthly magazine

1 / 3 明 拼音 míng ㄇㄧㄥˊ

正體字	簡體字	手 寫
明	明	明

筆 順
明 明
明 明
明 明
明
明

甲骨文	金 文	小 篆
𣇰	𣇰	𣆶

🔔 清楚知道：to know clearly

明白：to understand

你的心意我明白了。
I know what you're trying to say.

🔔 次：next

明天：tomorrow

不要為明天擔憂。
Tomorrow will take care of itself.

明年：next year

1 / 4 朋 拼音 péng ㄆㄥˊ

正體字	簡體字	手 寫
朋	朋	朋

筆 順
朋 朋
朋 朋
朋 朋
朋 朋
朋

甲骨文	金 文	小 篆
拜	拜	𦝠

🔔 彼此友好的人：people who are nice to each other

朋友：friend

他是我的好朋友。
He is my good friend.

1 5 白　拼音　bái　ㄅㄞˊ

正體字	簡體字	手寫
白	白	白

甲骨文	金文	小篆

筆順
白
白
白
白
白

📖 像日光像下射之形，太陽的光為白：like the color of sunlight

🔔 雪花或乳汁那樣的顏色：the very light color of fresh snow or milk

白色：white

白宮：the White House

🔔 潔淨：clean

潔白：pure white

她穿白色的衣服很迷人。
She looks charming in white.

1 6 百　拼音　bǎi　ㄅㄞˇ

正體字	簡體字	手寫
百	百	百

甲骨文	金文	小篆

筆順
百　百
百　百
百

10 x 10
100

🔔 數量詞，是十的十倍。：百 is the number one hundred, or ten times ten.

一百元：a hundred dollars

他的身體十分健康，百病不侵。
He is so healthy that he is immune to many sicknesses.

① 7　千　拼音　qiān　ㄑㄧㄢ

正體字	簡體字	手 寫	筆 順
千	千	千	千 千 千

甲骨文	金 文	小 篆
𠂊	千	𠂤

🔔 數量詞，是百的十倍：千 is the number one thousand, i.e., ten hundred.

一千元：a thousand dollars

> 我花了一千元買這雙鞋子。
> This pair of shoes cost me one thousand dollars.

🔔 眾多：also indicates "many"

千言萬語：thousands and thousands of words

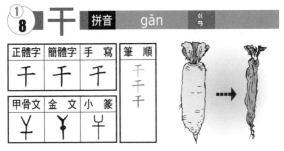

① 8　干　拼音　gān　ㄍㄢ

正體字	簡體字	手 寫	筆 順
干	干	干	干 干 干

甲骨文	金 文	小 篆
丫	𐤅	干

🔔 冒犯、觸犯：to offend, to invade

干預：to intervene

> 不要干預別人的事。
> Do not intervene in others' business.

🔔 相關：to have something to do with

相干：to be relevant

🔔 經脫水製成乾燥食品：to remove moisture and dry food

豆干：dried tofu

⑨ 天 拼音 tiān ㄊㄧㄢ

正體字	簡體字	手 寫	筆 順
天	天	天	天天天天

甲骨文	金 文	小 篆
𡗊	𡗊	天

※ 季節：season
　　春天：spring
※ 日：day
　　每天：every day

> 每天都很快樂。
> I am happy every day.

※ 氣候：climate or weather
　　天氣：weather
　　天空：the sky

⑩ 夫 拼音 fū ㄈㄨ

正體字	簡體字	手 寫	筆 順
夫	夫	夫	夫夫夫夫

甲骨文	金 文	小 篆
夫	夫	夫

※ 女子的配偶：a male spouse
　　丈夫：husband
※ 成年的人：adult
※ 農夫：farmer

> 她的丈夫是一位農夫。
> Her husband is a farmer.

①11 午 拼音 wǔ ㄨˇ

正體字	簡體字	手 寫	筆 順
午	午	午	午午午午

甲骨文	金 文	小 篆
𠂤	↑	午

🔔 白天十一點到一點：noon

   正午：noon

   午餐：lunch

> 今天我和朋友一起吃午餐。
> Today, I had lunch with a friend.

🔔 半夜：midnight

   午夜：midnight

①12 牛 拼音 niú ㄋㄧㄡˊ

正體字	簡體字	手 寫	筆 順
牛	牛	牛	牛牛牛牛

甲骨文	金 文	小 篆
ψ	ψ	半

🔔 牛：cow, ox, bull

   小牛：calf

   水牛：water buffalo

   牛仔：cowboy

   牛仔褲：jeans

🔔 固執：stubborn

   牛脾氣：stubbornness

> 不要理會他的牛脾氣。
> Ignore his stubbornness.

① 13 件 　拼音　 jiàn 　ㄐㄧㄢˋ

正體字	簡體字	手　寫	筆　順
件	件	件	件 件 件 件 件 件 件

甲骨文	金　文	小　篆
		件

🔔 物品、器具：articles, implements

零件：a part

🔔 計算事物的單位：a measure word

一件衣服：an item of clothing

他完成了一件很棒的作品。
He completed a wonderful piece.

① 14 來 　拼音　 lái 　ㄌㄞˊ

正體字	簡體字	手　寫	筆　順
來	来	來	來 來 來 來 來 來 來 來

甲骨文	金　文	小　篆
來	來	來

🔔 來往，與「去」相對：come, opposite of "go"

回來：come back

來去匆匆：come and go in haste

來來往往：come and go

來回車票：return ticket

他來了。
Here he comes.

🔔 下一次的：next

來年：next year

1 / 15 ー 拼音 yī ／

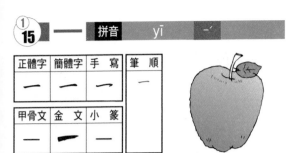

正體字	簡體字	手 寫	筆 順
一	一	一	一

甲骨文	金 文	小 篆
一	一	

◌ 數量詞「一」：one

　一個：a, an

　一個蘋果：an apple

　第一個：first

　一月是一年中的第一個月。
　January is the first month of the year.

◌ 代表相同的意思：also means "the same"

　一樣：the same

◌ 一寸光陰一寸金：Time is money.

1 / 16 十 拼音 shí ㄕ／

正體字	簡體字	手 寫	筆 順
十	十	十	十

甲骨文	金 文	小 篆

◌ 數量詞：ten

　十隻鳥：ten birds

　十誡：the Ten Commandments

◌ 完美：Ten connotes of "being perfect".

　十全十美：to be perfect

　世界上很少有十全十美的人。
　Few people in the world are perfect.

◌ 紅十字會：Red Cross

① 17 二 拼音 èr ㄦˋ

正體字	簡體字	手 寫	筆 順
二	二	二	二 二

甲骨文	金 文	小 篆
一	二	一

數量詞「二」：the number two.

二月：February

> 二月是一年中的第二個月。
> February is the second month of the year.

次序排第二的：second

第二名：the second place

① 18 工 拼音 gōng ㄍㄨㄥ

正體字	簡體字	手 寫	筆 順
工	工	工	工 工 工

甲骨文	金 文	小 篆
工	工	工

精緻、精巧：delicate

工整：neat

> 他寫字很工整。
> His handwriting is neat.

職業：career

工作：a job

從事勞動生產的人：worker, laborer

工人：a worker

① 19 三 拼音 sān ㄙㄢ

正體字	簡體字	手 寫	筆 順
三	三	三	三三三

甲骨文	金 文	小 篆
三	三	三

🔔 數量詞「三」：three

　　三張桌子：three tables

🔔 次序排第三的：third

> 三月是一年中的第三個月。
> March is the third month of the year.

　　第三排：the third row

🔔 **三國誌**：The History of the Three kingdoms

① 20 王 拼音 wáng ㄨㄤˊ

正體字	簡體字	手 寫	筆 順
王	王	王	王王王王

甲骨文	金 文	小 篆
大	王	王

🔔 古代一國君王的稱號，現代有些國家仍用
　　這種稱號：king, ruler

　　國王：king

　　王子：prince

　　王朝：dynasty

> 國王很富有。
> The king was very rich.

🔔 技藝超群的人：a highly skilled person

　　歌王：somebody who is great at singing

1/21 玉 拼音 yù ㄩˋ

正體字	簡體字	手 寫	筆 順
玉	玉	玉	玉 玉 玉 玉 玉

甲骨文	金 文	小 篆
丰	王	王

🔔 玉：jade

　玉鐲子：jade bracelet

　這是我剛買的玉鐲子。
　This is the jade bracelet that I just bought.

🔔 形容白淨、美好：white and beautiful

　玉手：slender white hand (of a beautiful woman)

🔔 珍貴的、美好：delicacy

　錦衣玉食：brocades and delicacies

1/22 主 拼音 zhǔ ㄓㄨˇ

正體字	簡體字	手 寫	筆 順
主	主	主	主 主 主 主 主

甲骨文	金 文	小 篆
		坐

🔔 相對於賓客而言：host

　主人：host

　他是昨晚餐宴的主人。
　He was the host of yesterday's dinner party.

🔔 負責：being responsible for something

　主辦者：host, sponsor

🔔 權力或財務的擁有者：lord, owner

　地主：landlord

正體字	簡體字	手 寫	筆 順
口	口	口	口 口 口

甲骨文	金 文	小 篆
凵	凵	凵

①23　口　拼音　kǒu　ㄎㄡ

🔔 嘴巴：the mouth

　　可口：delicious

> 這道菜很美味可口。
> This dish is delicious.

　　張口：open the mouth
　　口琴：harmonica
　　口試：oral test
　　口紅：lipstick

🔔 出入口：exit, entrance, doorway

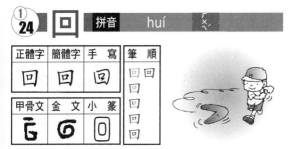

正體字	簡體字	手 寫	筆 順
回	回	回	回 回 回 回 回 回

甲骨文	金 文	小 篆
ᓂ	ᗉ	回

①24　回　拼音　huí　ㄏㄨㄟ

🔔 轉：to turn

　　回首：look back
　　返回：to return
　　回家：go back home

> 我每天晚上六點半回家。
> I get home from work every evening at 6:30.

　　回覆：to reply
　　回電：to call back

1/25 木 拼音 mù ㄇㄨˋ

正體字	簡體字	手 寫	筆 順
木	木	木	木 木 木 木

甲骨文	金 文	小 篆

木：tree, wood, timber

樹木：tree

用木材製成的：something that is made of wood

木椅：wooden chairs

> 這張木椅坐起來很舒適。
> This wooden chair is comfortable.

木造：wooden

麻木：numb

1/26 本 拼音 běn ㄅㄣˇ

正體字	簡體字	手 寫	筆 順
本	本	本	本 本 本 本 本

甲骨文	金 文	小 篆
		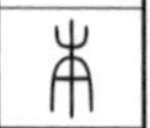

在「木」字加上一條線，是草木的根。：a line at the bottom of 木 makes a new character 本, which means root.

根本：basis

基本：base

量詞：a measure word

五本書：five books

> 上個月我讀了五本書。
> I read five books last month.

①27 林 拼音 lín ㄌㄧㄣˊ

正體字	簡體字	手寫	筆順
林	林	林	林 林 林林 林林 林林 林 林

甲骨文	金文	小篆
林	林	林

📖 林：forest, woods

森林：forest

> 這片森林很美。
> The forest is very beautiful.

📖 姓氏：a surname

📖 林林總總：numerous; many; multitudinous.

林立：stand in a great numbers; a forest of...

①28 森 拼音 sēn ㄙㄣ

正體字	簡體字	手寫	筆順
森	森	森	森 森 森 森 森 森 森 森 森 森 森

甲骨文	金文	小篆
森		森

📖 有很多的「木」，表示樹木濃密的樣子。：A lot of "trees" means forest.

森林：forest

> 這座森林是野生動物的樂園。
> This forest is a paradise for wild animals.

📖 陰森：gloomy

① 29　心

| 拼音 | xīn | ㄒㄧㄣ |

正體字	簡體字	手　寫	筆　順
心	心	心	心心心心

甲骨文	金　文	小　篆
♥	♥	心

🔔 心：heart

　　心臟：heart

🔔 用來表示思想或感情：thoughts, emotions

　　傷心：broken-hearted

　　全心全意：with all one's heart

> 我全心全意愛我的家人。
> I love my family with all my heart.

🔔 平面或物體的中央或內部：the center of an object

　　圓心：the center of a circle

① 30　必

| 拼音 | bì | ㄅㄧˋ |

正體字	簡體字	手　寫	筆　順
必	必	必	必必必必必

甲骨文	金　文	小　篆
弋	弌	悉

🔔 一定的意思：must, be sure to

　　必須：must

> 這件事情必須在今天完成。
> This has to be done today.

　　必定：be sure to

　　必要：necessary, necessarily

　　必需品：necessities

　　必要條件：requirement

正體字	簡體字	手寫	筆順
五	五	五	五 五 五 五

甲骨文	金文	小篆
✕	✕	✕

拼音　wǔ　ㄨˇ

①31　五

🔔 數量詞「五」：the number five

　五個杯子：five cups

🔔 次序排第五的：fifth

> 五月是一年中的第五個月。
> May is the fifth month of the year.

　第五個人：the fifth person

> 我是第五個進教室的人。
> I was the fifth one to enter the classroom.

　五星級：five-star

🔔 五重奏：quintet

2月
February

②1 伍 | 拼音 | wǔ | ㄨˇ

正體字	簡體字	手 寫	筆 順
伍	伍	伍	伍伍 伍 伍 伍 伍

甲骨文	金 文	小 篆
		伍

🔔 古代軍隊的編制單位，以五人為一伍：
the basic five-man unit of the army in ancient
China

隊伍：troops, ranks

軍隊：army

入伍：to enlist into the army

🔔 姓氏：a surname

> 伍先生在海軍服役。
> Mr. Wu serves in the navy.

②2 六 | 拼音 | liù | ㄌㄧㄡˋ

正體字	簡體字	手 寫	筆 順
六	六	六	六 六 六 六

甲骨文	金 文	小 篆
	介	𡴆

🔔 數詞「六」：the number six

六間房子：six houses

> 我擁有六間房子。
> I own six houses.

🔔 次序排第六的：sixth

> 六月是一年中的第六個月。
> June is the sixth month of the year.

第六個人：the sixth person

② 3 陸

拼音	lù	ㄌ ㄨˋ

正體字	簡體字	手 寫	筆 順
陸	陆	陸	陸陸陸 陸陸 陸陸 陸陸 陸陸

甲骨文	金 文	小 篆
		陸

📖 高出水面的平地：land as opposed to water

登陸：to land

> 太空人登陸月球。
> The astronaut landed on the moon.

陸地：land

陸橋：land bridge

📖 姓氏：a surname

② 4 大

拼音	dà	ㄉ ㄚˋ

正體字	簡體字	手 寫	筆 順
大	大	大	大 大 大

甲骨文	金 文	小 篆
大	大	大

📖 像是一個正面站立的的人：大 looks like a standing figure

📖 形容面積、深度、強度較強：big, huge, large, great

大雨：heavy rain

> 大雨造成河水暴漲。
> The heavy rain caused the river to rise suddenly.

📖 **大約**：approximately

②5 小 拼音 xiǎo ㄒㄧㄠˇ

正體字	簡體字	手寫	筆順
小	小	小	小 小 小

甲骨文	金文	小篆
⺌	⺌	川

🔔 微小，與「大」相對：small, the opposite of big

小狗：puppy

小馬：pony

> 小馬很可愛。
> That pony is adorable.

🔔 邪惡：evil

小人：evil people

🔔 謹慎：to be cautious

小心：to be careful

②6 犬 拼音 quǎn ㄑㄩㄢˇ

正體字	簡體字	手寫	筆順
犬	犬	犬	犬 犬 犬 犬

甲骨文	金文	小篆
犬	犬	犬

🔔 狗：a dog

惡犬：a mean dog

> 小心惡犬攻擊。
> Be careful. That vicious dog could attack.

🔔 稱自己的兒子為「小犬」。：humble way of referring to your own son

🔔 犬齒（人的）：canine tooth

2/7 太 拼音 tài ㄊㄞ

正體字	簡體字	手寫	筆順
太	太	太	太太大太

甲骨文	金文	小篆

🔔 過多的意思：too much, very

太熱：too hot

太高：too tall

你太多話了（囉嗦）。
You talk too much.

2/8 丁 拼音 dīng ㄉㄧㄥ

正體字	簡體字	手寫	筆順
丁	丁	丁	丁丁

甲骨文	金文	小篆
☐	●	个

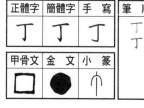

📖 原本是釘子的意思，所以字形像是俯視的釘頭：Originally 丁 meant nail.

🔔 成年男子：adult male

男丁：man

壯丁：a stong man

🔔 管理園圃，培植花木的人：a man who takes care of gardens and flowers

園丁：a gardener

②9 叮　拼音　dīng　ㄉㄧㄥ

正體字	簡體字	手　寫	筆　順
叮	叮	叮	叮 叮 叮 叮 叮

甲骨文	金　文	小　篆

🔔 指昆蟲用口器螫咬人或動物：to sting or bite (of insects)

蚊子叮咬：a mosquito bite

小心蚊子叮咬。
Be careful not to be bitten by mosquitoes.

🔔 再三吩咐：to urge again and again

叮嚀：to exhort, urge

🔔 叮噹：dingdong (of a bell)

②10 力　拼音　lì　ㄌㄧˋ

正體字	簡體字	手　寫	筆　順
力	力	力	力 力

甲骨文	金　文	小　篆
ㄑ	㇋	ㄌ

🔔 運動所產生的效能：energy, potency

力氣：strength

用力：exert one's strength

我用力的拉繩子。
I pulled on the rope hard.

🔔 一個人的本領：a person's ability

能力：ability

2/11 刀　拼音　dāu　ㄉㄠ

正體字	簡體字	手　寫	筆　順
刀	刀	刀	刀 刀

甲骨文	金　文	小　篆
ゟ	ゟ	刀

兵器：weapons
　刀劍：knife, sword

用來切、削、剪……等的工具：a tool used to cut, to slice, or to pare
　菜刀：kitchen knife
　剪刀：scissors

> 拿剪刀給別人要注意安全。
> Be careful when handing scissors to others.

2/12 分　拼音　fēn　ㄈㄣ

正體字	簡體字	手　寫	筆　順
分	分	分	分 分 分 分

甲骨文	金　文	小　篆
八刀	八刀	八刀

表示用刀將一件物品分開成兩個部分，整個字表示用刀剖開東西的樣子：分 indicates to cut an object into parts with a knife (刀).
　分開：to part
　分割：to cut apart

計算時間的單位：a unit of time
　分鐘：minute

> 再過五分鐘就要下課了。
> The class will be over in 5 more minutes.

② 13 份 　拼音　fèn　ㄈㄣˋ

正體字	簡體字	手　寫	筆　順
份	份	份	份份 份 份 份

甲骨文	金　文	小　篆
		𣬛

指整體中的部分：a share or part of something

股份：stock share

計算事物的單位：a measure unit

一份報紙：a piece of newspaper

兩份薪水：two salaries

公司只訂一份報紙。
The company only subscribes to one newspaper.

② 14 人 　拼音　rén　ㄖㄣˊ

正體字	簡體字	手　寫	筆　順
人	人	人	人 人

甲骨文	金　文	小　篆
𠃛	𠃌	𠄠

人類：human beings, humanity, mankind

男人：man

女人：woman

某種類型或身分的人：a person of a certain category or position

主持人：host, hostess

她在電台擔任節目主持人。
She is the hostess of a radio program.

人人平等：All men are equal.

②15 入 拼音 rù ㄖㄨˋ

正體字	簡體字	手寫	筆順
入	入	入	入入

甲骨文	金文	小篆
入	入	入

🔔 由外部進到內部：to come or go into

入入 進入：get into; enter

> 進入校園要先登記身分。
> You have to sign in before entering the campus.

🔔 沈浸、深透：immerse

入迷：be fascinated; be charmed

🔔 收進：incorporate

收入：income

入不敷出：to be unable to make ends meet

②16 音 拼音 yīn ㄧㄣ

正體字	簡體字	手寫	筆順
音	音	音	音音音音音

甲骨文	金文	小篆
	音	音

🔔 任何的聲音：any sound

噪音：noise

> 請不要製造噪音。
> Please do not make any noise.

回音：reply

🔔 消息：news

佳音：good news

② 17 唱　拼音　chàng　ㄔㄤ

正體字	簡體字	手　寫	筆　順
唱	唱	唱	唱 唱 唱 唱 唱 唱 唱 唱 唱

甲骨文	金　文	小　篆
		唱

🔔 發出歌聲：to sing

　　唱歌：to sing

　　合唱團：chorus

　　我是合唱團的團員。
　　I am a member of a choir.

🔔 高聲呼叫：call out with a loud voice

　　唱名：rollcall

🔔 唱反調：to express an opposing view

② 18 可　拼音　kě　ㄎㄜ

正體字	簡體字	手　寫	筆　順
可	可	可	可 可 可 可

甲骨文	金　文	小　篆
丂	可	可

🔔 表示肯定：positive

　　許可：to permit

🔔 值得、堪：worthy

　　可敬：worthy of respect

🔔 可人：pleasant, charming

　　可人兒：a nice person

　　她是一位很有魅力的可人兒。
　　She is a charming girl.

2/19 哥

| 拼音 | gē | ㄍㄜ |

正體字	簡體字	手寫	筆順
哥	哥	哥	哥哥 哥哥 哥哥 哥哥 哥
甲骨文	金文	小篆	
		哥	

表示對兄長的稱呼：a way to address one's elder brother

哥哥：elder brother

我和哥哥的感情很好。
I am close to my older brother.

哥兒們：buddies

2/20 河

| 拼音 | hé | ㄏㄜ |

正體字	簡體字	手寫	筆順
河	河	河	河河 河河 河河 河 河
甲骨文	金文	小篆	
𣲘		河	

水流的通稱：a general name for rivers and streams

河流：the river
黃河：the Yellow River
河邊：river bank

河邊風景很美。
The scenery along the river is beautiful.

銀河：the Milky Way

②21 何 | 拼音 | hé | ㄏㄜˊ

正體字	簡體字	手寫	筆順
何	何	何	何何 何何 何何 何

甲骨文	金文	小篆
(甲骨文字形)	何	何

☼ 如何：how, how about...

我不知道應該如何解決這個問題。
I have no idea how to solve this problem.

☼ 為什麼：why

為何：For what reason?

☼ 姓氏：a surname

何先生：Mr. He

②22 中 | 拼音 | zhōng | ㄓㄨㄥ

正體字	簡體字	手寫	筆順
中	中	中	中 中 中 中

甲骨文	金文	小篆
中	中	中

☼ 距離四方或兩端相等的部位：The distances from a point/part to the four directions or both ends are the same.

中央：center

☼ 裡面：inside, interior

中間：middle

☼ 得：to get (pronounced zhòng ㄓㄨㄥˋ)

中獎：to win a prize

中獎是一件喜事。
Winning a prize is a happy occasion.

2/23 申 拼音 shēn ㄕㄣ

正體字	簡體字	手 寫	筆 順
申	申	申	申 申 申 申

甲骨文	金 文	小 篆
⌇	⌇	㽴

🔔 陳述、說明：to state, express, explain

申訴：to complain

🔔 申請：to apply for

申請人：applicant

申請書：application

2/24 上 拼音 shàng ㄕㄤ

正體字	簡體字	手 寫	筆 順
上	上	上	上 上 上

甲骨文	金 文	小 篆
⌣	二	丄

🔔 物體的表面、高處或邊側：on top, above

山上：on the mountain

🔔 去、到：to go to, to attend

上學：go to school

🔔 先前的：previous, last

上個月：last month

上個月我非常忙碌。
I was very busy last month.

2/25 下　拼音　xià　ㄒㄧㄚˋ

正體字	簡體字	手　寫	筆　順
下	下	下	下下下

甲骨文	金　文	小　篆
⌒	二	下

🔔 低處、底部。與上相對：at the bottom, the opposite of "above"

底下：beneath

🔔 下班：to get off work

🔔 時間或次序在後的：next

下次：next time

下一代：the next generation

2/26 卡　拼音　kǎ　ㄎㄚˇ

正體字	簡體字	手　寫	筆　順
卡	卡	卡	卡卡卡卡卡

甲骨文	金　文	小　篆

🔔 被夾住：to be stuck

卡住：stuck

我的車子被石頭卡住了。
My car got stuck in some rocks.

🔔 硬紙片：cardboard

生日卡：birthday card

🔔 派兵駐守的關口：a pass which is garrisoned by an army

關卡：customs pass, outpost, checkpoint

🔔 卡通：cartoon

2/27 車

正體字	簡體字	手寫
車	车	車

甲骨文	金文	小篆
(甲骨文)	車	車

筆順
車車車車車車

🔔 陸地上有輪子的交通工具：vehicles

　　汽車：car

　　車站：bus station

> 我買一輛腳踏車給自己。
> I bought a bike for myself.

🔔 利用輪軸所轉動的機械：A machine which uses wheels and axles to move.

　　風車：windmill

　　水車：water wheel

2/28 山

正體字	簡體字	手寫
山	山	山

甲骨文	金文	小篆
(甲骨文)	(金文)	山

筆順
山山山

🔔 陸地上高起的部分：the higher parts of the land

　　高山：high mountains

> 攀登高山是一種挑戰。
> Climbing high mountains is a challenge.

🔔 山村：mountain village

*3*月
March

③1 出 　拼音　chū　ㄔㄨ

正體字	簡體字	手寫	筆　順
出	出	出	出 出 出 出 出

甲骨文	金　文	小　篆
（甲骨文字形）	（金文字形）	（小篆字形）

出：to go out, to occur, to show, to produce

出門：to go out

出生：to be born

出局：to eliminate, to be out (in baseball)

出席：to attend

今天我出席了一場學術研討會。
I attended an academic seminar today.

拿出：to take out

請拿出您的證件。
Please show me your ID.

③2 水 　拼音　shuǐ　ㄕㄨㄟˇ

正體字	簡體字	手寫	筆　順
水	水	水	水 水 水 水

甲骨文	金　文	小　篆
（甲骨文字形）	（金文字形）	（小篆字形）

河流：river

水流：current

河水：river water

水上人家：boat dwellers

這裡的河水很清澈。
The river here is very clear.

液體：liquid or fluid

墨水：ink

藥水：liquid medicine

水果：fruit

3/3 火 拼音 huǒ ㄏㄨㄛˇ

正體字	簡體字	手寫	筆順
火	火	火	火火火火

甲骨文	金文	小篆
	火	火

物體燃燒時產生的光和熱：the light and heat produced from the combustion of materials

火光：firelight

紅色的：red

火紅：flaming red

發脾氣：get angry

發火：get angry

他經常發火。
He gets angry a lot.

3/4 內 拼音 nèi ㄋㄟˋ

正體字	簡體字	手寫	筆順
內	內	內	內內內內

甲骨文	金文	小篆
	內	內

從門進入房子的內部：內 is a pictograph of walking into a house (through the door).

房子裡面：inside a house

室內：indoor, interior

我在室內休息。
I took a rest indoors.

室內遊戲：indoor games

內衣：underwear

³⁄₅ 外 　拼音　wài　ㄨㄞˋ

正體字	簡體字	手寫	筆順
外	外	外	外外外外外

甲骨文	金文	小篆
	ᗩᏐ	外

🔔 不屬於某一定的範圍內均稱為外。相對於「內」而言外：not belonging within a certain range, opposite of「內」

　門外：outside the door

> 她把狗拴在門外。
> She tied up a guard dog outside her house.

🔔 非自己所在或所屬的：a place other than the one in which you are located or belong

　外幣：foreign currency

³⁄₆ 夕 　拼音　xì　ㄒㄧˋ

正體字	簡體字	手寫	筆順
夕	夕	夕	夕夕夕

甲骨文	金文	小篆
ⅅ	ⅅ	⅌

🔔 黃昏、傍晚：dusk or twilight

　夕陽：the setting sun

> 我喜歡欣賞夕陽。
> I like to enjoy sunsets.

🔔 夜晚：night

　朝夕相處：to be together from morning to night

正體字	簡體字	手 寫	筆 順
多	多	多	多 多 多 多 多

甲骨文	金 文	小 篆

📖 把兩個夕放在一起組成的多字，意思是很多：putting two 「夕」s together constitutes 「多」, which means many (night after night).

多元論：pluralism

🔔 表示東西的數量很大：a large quantity

好多：many

🔔 多謝：Thanks a lot.

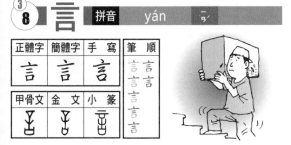

正體字	簡體字	手 寫	筆 順
言	言	言	言 言 言 言 言

甲骨文	金 文	小 篆

🔔 說、講：to speak

苦不堪言：indescribable misery

🔔 學說、言論：schools, doctrine

一家之言：theory of one school

言行一致：match word to deed

🔔 語言：language

學中國語言很有趣。
Learning Chinese is interesting.

³⁄₉ 信 拼音 xìn ㄒㄧㄣ

正體字	簡體字	手 寫	筆 順
信	信	信	信 信 信 信 信 信 信 信 信

甲骨文	金 文	小 篆
		信

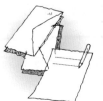

🔔 誠實不欺騙：honest, not deceitful

誠信：good faith

🔔 不懷疑：to not doubt

相信：to believe

> 我相信他說的都是實話。
> I believe all he said is true.

🔔 書札：letter

寫信：to write a letter

³⁄₁₀ 目 拼音 mù ㄇㄨˋ

正體字	簡體字	手 寫	筆 順
目	目	目	目 目 目 目 目

甲骨文	金 文	小 篆
目	目	目

🔔 眼睛：the eyes

目光：eyesight

🔔 名稱、標題：name, title

題目：title, topic, theme

🔔 目前：at present

> 目前黃金很值錢。
> At present, gold is valuable.

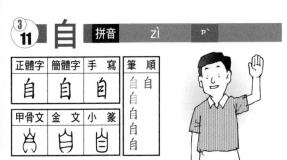

正體字	簡體字	手 寫	筆 順
自	自	自	自自自自自

甲骨文	金 文	小 篆

🔔 本人、己身：oneself

自己：oneself

自願：volunteer

我自願到偏遠的地方服務。
I volunteered to serve in a remote area.

自作自受：reap what one has sown

🔔 從：from, since

自古以來：since ancient times to the present

🔔 自由：freedom

自由市場：the free market

正體字	簡體字	手 寫	筆 順
文	文	文	文文文文

甲骨文	金 文	小 篆

🔔 文字：character, written language

英文：English

🔔 文章：article

散文：essay

🔔 溫和、優雅：gentle, mild, elegant

斯文：refined

他很斯文。
He has very refined manners.

正體字	簡體字	手 寫	筆 順
貝	贝	貝	貝貝貝貝貝貝貝

甲骨文	金 文	小 篆

③ 13 貝　拼音　bèi　ㄅㄟˋ

有甲殼的軟體動物：貝 indicates shellfish
　　貝殼：shell
　　貝類：mollusks
姓氏：surname

貝小姐在海邊撿貝殼。
Miss Bei picked up shells on the seashore.

③ 14 買　拼音　mǎi　ㄇㄞˇ

正體字	簡體字	手 寫	筆 順
買	买	買	買買買買買買買

甲骨文	金 文	小 篆

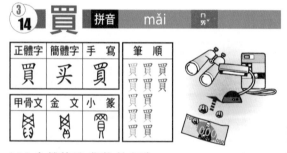

拿錢換取貨物的行為：to exchange money for goods
　　買書：buy books

他喜歡閱讀和買書。
He likes reading and buying books.

正體字	簡體字	手　寫	筆　順
賣	卖	賣	賣賣賣賣 賣賣賣賣 賣賣賣

甲骨文	金　文	小　篆
	𧶠	𧶠

🔔 出售貨物：to sell products

　 賣車：to sell cars

🔔 出賣：to betray

　 賣國賊：traitor

🔔 炫耀、顯露：to show off, become visible

　 賣弄：show off

> 他喜歡賣弄自己的口才。
> He likes to show off his eloquence.

正體字	簡體字	手　寫	筆　順
毋	毋	毋	毋 毋 毋 毋

甲骨文	金　文	小　篆
		毋

🔔 不、不要、沒有：no, do not

　 毋須：no need to...

> 這個問題他會解決，毋須擔心。
> Don't worry. He will solve this problem.

③ 17 母 拼音 mǔ ㄇㄨˇ

正體字	簡體字	手寫	筆順
母	母	母	母 母 母 母

甲骨文	金文	小篆
(甲骨文字形)	(金文字形)	(小篆字形)

🔔 母親：mother

> 文女士是一位偉大的母親。
> Mrs. Wen is a great mother.

🔔 雌性的：female

母雞：hen

母狗：bitch

母馬：mare

母豬：sow

母牛：cow

③ 18 每 拼音 měi ㄇㄟˇ

正體字	簡體字	手寫	筆順
每	每	每	每 每 每 每 每

甲骨文	金文	小篆
(甲骨文字形)	(金文字形)	(小篆字形)

🔔 經常：often

每次：every time

🔔 各個：each

每個人：everybody

> 這部電影適合每個人觀賞。
> This movie is suitable for everybody.

🔔 天天：each day

每天：every day

③ 海 拼音 hǎi ㄏㄞˇ
19

正體字	簡體字	手寫	筆順
海	海	海	海海 海海 海海 海海 海海

甲骨文	金文	小篆
	𣲘	𣲘

🔔 大海：the sea
　　海洋：ocean

　　他喜歡在海中游泳。
　　He likes to swim in the sea.

🔔 海邊的沙地：an area of sand next to a sea
　　海灘：the beach

③ 左 拼音 zuǒ ㄗㄨㄛˇ
20

正體字	簡體字	手寫	筆順
左	左	左	左 左 左 左 左

甲骨文	金文	小篆
𠂇	𠂇	𠂇

🔔 與「右」相對：the opposite of right
　　左邊：left side
　　左手：left hand

　　他習慣用左手寫字。
　　He is used to using his left hand to write.

🔔 違背：to go against
　　意見相左：have different opinions
🔔 不正當的：improper
　　旁門左道：heresy

③21 右　拼音　yòu　ㄧㄡˋ

正體字	簡體字	手　寫	筆　順
右	右	右	右 右 右 右

甲骨文	金　文	小　篆
	局	司

☆ 與「左」相對：the opposite of left

　　右邊：right side

　　右手：right hand

☆ 左右為難：in a dilemma

> 這件事讓他左右為難，很難下決定。
> This has put him in a dilemma. It is very difficult for him to make a decision.

③22 手　拼音　shǒu　ㄕㄡˇ

正體字	簡體字	手　寫	筆　順
手	手	手	手 手 手 手

甲骨文	金　文	小　篆
	￥	￥

☆ 手：hand

　　右手：right hand

> 我用右手寫字。
> I write with my right hand.

☆ 助手、幫手：assistant, helper

☆ 與手有關的：to have something to do with the hands

　　手杖：walking stick

3/23 打 | 拼音 dǎ | ㄉㄚˇ

正體字	簡體字	手寫	筆　順
打	打	打	打 打 打 打

甲骨文	金　文	小　篆
		扚

🔔 敲擊：to strike

　　打鼓：to play the drum

🔔 攻擊、戰鬥：to attack, to fight

　　打架：to fight

　　打仗：to battle

他喜歡打架鬧事。
He likes fighting and making trouble.

3/24 九 | 拼音 jiǔ | ㄐㄧㄡˇ

正體字	簡體字	手寫	筆　順
九	九	九	九 九

甲骨文	金　文	小　篆
ξ	ξ	九

🔔 數量詞「九」：the number nine

　　九輛車：nine cars

🔔 次序排第九的：九 is also an ordinal number, the ninth

　　第九排：the ninth row

我坐在第九排聆聽音樂會。
I sat in the ninth row at the concert.

③25 久 拼音 jiǔ ㄐㄧㄡˇ

正體字	簡體字	手 寫	筆 順
久	久	久	久久久

甲骨文	金 文	小 篆
		弋

📖 人的兩腿之間的距離：stride

🔔 時間長遠：for a long time

　　長久：for a long time

　　永久：eternal

🔔 經歷時間的長短：a length of time

　　多久：how long

> 他出去多久了？
> How long has he been out?

③26 父 拼音 fù ㄈㄨˋ

正體字	簡體字	手 寫	筆 順
父	父	父	父父父父

甲骨文	金 文	小 篆
	乀	弌

🔔 對爸爸的稱呼：a male parent

　　父親（爸爸）：father (dad)

> 我的父親是一位仁慈的長者。
> My father is a kind older man.

🔔 國父：the father of a country

🔔 祖父：paternal grandfather

　　外祖父：maternal grandfather

正體字	簡體字	手寫	筆順
爸	爸	爸	爸爸爸爸爸爸爸
甲骨文	金文	小篆	

爸爸：dad, father

他是兩個孩子的爸爸。
He is the father of two children.

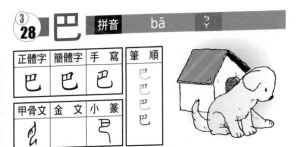

正體字	簡體字	手寫	筆順
巴	巴	巴	巴巴巴巴
甲骨文	金文	小篆	

尾巴：tail

狗搖著尾巴迎接主人。
The dog wagged its tail as it welcomed its master.

因乾燥、黏稠而凝結成塊的物體：
something that forms as a result of drying up
泥巴：mud

③ 29 共 拼音 gòng ㄍㄨㄥˋ

正體字	簡體字	手　寫	筆　順
共	共	共	共 共 共 共 共

甲骨文	金　文	小　篆
	共	共

🔔 一同、相同：together, common

共同：jointly

共生：coexist, symbiosis

🔔 總計：to total

總共：in total

🔔 眾人共有的：shared by all

公共：public

公共場所不宜大聲喧嘩。
It is not appropriate to yell in public.

共產主義：communism

③ 30 女 拼音 nǚ ㄋㄩˇ

正體字	簡體字	手　寫	筆　順
女	女	女	女 女 女

甲骨文	金　文	小　篆
女	女	女

🔔 婦女：woman

女性：female

女兒：daughter

獨生女：an only daughter

生兒育女：bear and raise sons and daughters

🔔 女性的：female, woman

女教師：a female teacher

這所小學的女教師較多。
There are more female teachers in this elementary school.

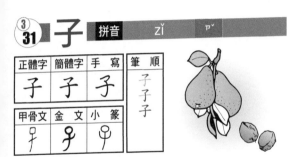

正體字	簡體字	手　寫	筆　順
子	子	子	子 子 子

甲骨文	金　文	小　篆
㝢	㝢	㝢

兒子：son

獨生子：an only son

我是家裡的獨生子。
I am the only son in my family.

子孫：offspring

植物的果實、種子或動物的卵：fruits or seeds of plants, or eggs

魚子：fish eggs

孔子：Confucius

孟子：Mencius

$4_{月}$
April

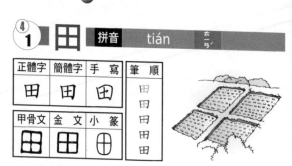

④1 田 拼音 tián ㄊㄧㄢˊ

正體字	簡體字	手 寫	筆 順
田	田	田	田 田 田 田 田

甲骨文	金 文	小 篆
田	田	田

☀ 用來耕種農作物的地方：a field for farming

田地：field

☀ 可開採某些資源的地帶：field with resources that can be mined

鹽田：salt field

☀ 姓氏：a surname

> 田先生擁有這片田地。
> Mr. Tian owns this field.

④2 男 拼音 nán ㄋㄢˊ

正體字	簡體字	手 寫	筆 順
男	男	男	男 男 男 男 男 男

甲骨文	金 文	小 篆
男	男	男

☀ 在田地中勞動的男子：This character means men working hard in the field.

> 男女平等。
> Men and women are equal.

男性：male

男朋友：boyfriend

> 他是我的男朋友。
> He is my boyfriend.

☀ 兒子：son

④3 好  拼音 hǎu ㄏㄠˇ

正體字	簡體字	手寫	筆順
好	好	好	好好好好好

甲骨文	金文	小篆

🔔 美好：fine, nice

我們過了一個美好的假日。
We had a nice holiday.

好好先生：a yes-man

好人好事：good personalities and good deeds

🔔 友愛：friendly, kind

友好：friendly

🔔 完成：finished

做好了：It is done.

④4 馬 拼音 mǎ ㄇㄚˇ

正體字	簡體字	手寫	筆順
馬	马	馬	馬馬馬馬馬馬馬馬

甲骨文	金文	小篆

🔔 馬匹：horse

小馬：pony

斑馬：zebra

🔔 馬拉松：marathon

🔔 馬上：at once

🔔 姓氏：a surname

馬校長家裡養了一匹小馬。
Principal Ma has a pony.

④5 嗎 拼音 ma ˙ㄇㄚ

正體字	簡體字	手 寫
嗎	吗	嗎

甲骨文	金 文	小 篆

筆 順
嗎 嗎 嗎
嗎 嗎 嗎
嗎 嗎 嗎
嗎 嗎
嗎 嗎

🔔 這個字通常放在句尾，表示疑問的語氣。：Usually, 「嗎」is put at the end of a sentence to make a question.

你好嗎？：How are you?

滿意嗎？：Satisfied?

> 這件事你滿意嗎？
> Are you satisfied with this?

④6 媽 拼音 mā ㄇㄚ

正體字	簡體字	手 寫
媽	妈	媽

甲骨文	金 文	小 篆

筆 順
媽 媽 媽
媽 媽 媽
媽 媽 媽
媽 媽
媽 媽

🔔 對母親的稱謂：mother (informal)

媽媽：mom, mother

> 我有一位溫柔的媽媽。
> My mom is gentle.

4/7 土　拼音 tǔ　ㄊㄨˇ

正體字	簡體字	手　寫	筆　順
土	土	土	土 土 土
甲骨文	金　文	小　篆	
		土	

土壤：soil; ground

泥土：mud; soil

我家後院的泥土冒出了綠芽。
A green sprout has come out from the soil in my backyard.

疆域：territory, domain

國土：territory

領土：land

4/8 也　拼音 yě　ㄧㄝˇ

正體字	簡體字	手　寫	筆　順
也	也	也	也 也 也
甲骨文	金　文	小　篆	

同樣：also

你知道，我也知道。
You know it. I also know it.

也許：perhaps

表示強調：to emphasize

再也不：not anymore, no more

我再也不會遲到了。
I won't be late anymore.

④9 地　拼音　dì　ㄉㄧˋ

正體字	簡體字	手寫	筆順
地	地	地	地地地地地地

甲骨文	金文	小篆
		墬

- 🔔 **大地**：ground; earth
  - **本地**：local
  - **地理**：geography
- 🔔 **目的地**：destination

> 這次旅遊的目的地是澳洲。
> The destination of this tour is Australia.

- 🔔 **地下**：underground
  - **地下鐵道**：subway
  - **地下室**：basement
- 🔔 **地震**：earthquake

④10 不　拼音　bù　ㄅㄨˋ

正體字	簡體字	手寫	筆順
不	不	不	不不不不

甲骨文	金文	小篆
🄯	🄯	🄯

- 🔔 表示否定：「不」 expresses negation.
  - **不要**：do not
  - **不是**：no

> 請你不要再說了。
> Please stop talking.

> 我不介意。
> I don't mind.

- 🔔 **不公平**：to be unfair

④ 11 才 | 拼音 | cái | ㄘㄞˊ

正體字	簡體字	手寫	筆順
才	才	才	才 才 才

甲骨文	金文	小篆

🔔 **剛才**：just now

🔔 **有才能**：talented, gifted

天才：genius, gifted

才德：talent and virtue

他是個才德兼備之人。
He is the person who has both talent and virtue.

🔔 **僅有**：only

他才五歲。
He is just five.

④ 12 寸 | 拼音 | cùn | ㄘㄨㄣˋ

正體字	簡體字	手寫	筆順
寸	寸	寸	寸 寸 寸

甲骨文	金文	小篆

2decimeters

🔔 計算長度的單位，公寸的一寸等於10
公分：a unit for measuring length. One
decimeter is equal to 10 centimeters.

公寸：decimeter

🔔 形容非常小、短、少：「寸」is used to
describe something very small, short, and
few.

寸步不離：keep close, follow closely

④ 13 付 拼音 fù ㄈㄨˋ

正體字	簡體字	手 寫	筆 順
付	付	付	付 付 付 付 付

甲骨文	金 文	小 篆
	𡴀	𩇢

🔔 把一件東西交給另一個人：to hand over something

付錢：to pay for something

我購物用刷卡付錢。
I pay by credit card when shopping.

交付：to deliver

④ 14 片 拼音 piàn ㄆㄧㄢˋ

正體字	簡體字	手 寫	筆 順
片	片	片	片 片 片 片

甲骨文	金 文	小 篆
𤕦		𠂤

🔔 表示薄而扁平的東西：an object that is thin and flat

肉片：meat slice

🔔 計算單位的量詞：a measure word

一片土司：a slice of bread

🔔 名片：business card

這是我的名片，敬請指教。
This is my business card. Any advice will be appreciated.

4/15 北 | 拼音 | běi | ㄅㄟ

正體字	簡體字	手 寫	筆 順
北	北	北	北 北 北 北

甲骨文	金 文	小 篆
北	北	北

🔔 「南」的相對：the opposite of south

北方：north

北極：the North Pole

🔔 向北，表示行動的方向：northward (moving towards north)

北上：to go north

臺北101摩天樓在臺灣的北部。
The Taipei 101 skyscraper is situated in northern Taiwan.

4/16 南 | 拼音 | nán | ㄋㄢ

正體字	簡體字	手 寫	筆 順
南	南	南	南 南 南 南 南

甲骨文	金 文	小 篆
南	南	南

🔔 「北」的相對：the opposite of north

南方：south

往南走，可以到達海邊。
You can reach the beach from here by walking south.

🔔 南邊的：southern

南極：the South Pole

④ 17 化 拼音 huà ㄏㄨㄚˋ

正體字	簡體字	手寫	筆順
化	化	化	化 化 化 化

甲骨文	金文	小篆
𣏾	𠤎	𠤎

改變：to transform, to change

千變萬化：ever-changing

化粧舞會：masquerade party

千變萬化的魔術表演，令人驚嘆不已！
The magic show was fast-changing. It was amazing.

燒毀：to be burnt down

火化：cremation

化工：chemical engineering

④ 18 花 拼音 huā ㄏㄨㄚ

正體字	簡體字	手寫	筆順
花	花	花	花花 花花 花花 花

甲骨文	金文	小篆

花朵：the flower

我喜歡紅色的花朵。
I love red flowers.

耗費：to spend

花錢：to spend the money

我把錢花在買書上。
I spent my money on books.

巧妙：ingenious

花招：tricks

④
19 巾 | 拼音 | jīn | ㄐㄧㄣ

正體字	簡體字	手 寫	筆 順
巾	巾	巾	巾 巾 巾

甲骨文	金 文	小 篆
巾	巾	巾

🔔 手帕：handkerchief
　手巾：handkerchief
🔔 擦洗用的布：cloth for cleaning or drying
　毛巾：towel
🔔 纏繞用的布或裝飾品：cloth or decoration
　that can be wrapped around the neck or head
　圍巾：scarf

> 這是我親手編織的圍巾。
> This is the scarf that I knitted on my own.

④
20 布 | 拼音 | bù | ㄅㄨ

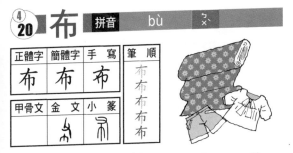

正體字	簡體字	手 寫	筆 順
布	布	布	布 布 布 布

甲骨文	金 文	小 篆
布	布	布

🔔 可作為衣物的材料：made of cotton, linen,
　silk, or wool
　棉布：cotton cloth
🔔 發表：to make known
　宣布：to announce
　發布：to release

> 氣象局發布海上颱風警報。
> The Bureau of Meteorology released a
> typhoon warning.

布告：bulletin

4/21 已 拼音 yǐ ㄧˇ

正體字	簡體字	手 寫	筆 順
已	已	已	已 已 已

甲骨文	金 文	小 篆

🔔 已經：already

已婚：married

他已是有婦之夫。
He is a married man.

🔔 開心不已：be continuously happy

得獎讓我開心不已！
I am very happy about winning the prize.

🔔 已成定局：The outcome is settled.

4/22 己 拼音 jǐ ㄐㄧˇ

正體字	簡體字	手 寫	筆 順
己	己	己	己 己 己

甲骨文	金 文	小 篆
己	己	己

🔔 自稱：a way to address oneself

自己：oneself

這是我自己的事情，請不用操心。
This is my business. You don't have to
worry about it.

自私者把自己的利益看得最重。
A selfish person puts self first.

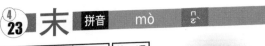

4/23 末 拼音 mò ㄇㄛˋ

正體字	簡體字	手 寫	筆 順
末	末	末	末 末 末 末 末

甲骨文	金 文	小 篆
	末	末

🔔 物體的尾端或頂端：end or the top of an object

末端：end, extremity

> 末班車即將開走。
> The last train (or bus) will be leaving soon.

🔔 碎屑、細粉：small pieces; fine powder

粉末：powder

🔔 事物的最後階段：the last/final stage of a thing

歲末：end of a year

4/24 未 拼音 wèi ㄨㄟˋ

正體字	簡體字	手 寫	筆 順
未	未	未	未 未 未 未 未

甲骨文	金 文	小 篆
未	未	未

🔔 中國時辰的名稱。大約下午一點到三點：the period between 1pm ~ 3pm in China's traditional way of dividing time

未時：the period of 1 pm to 3 pm

🔔 不、沒有：have not

未曾：never

🔔 將來：future

未來：future

4/25 味 | 拼音 | wèi | ㄨㄟˋ

正體字	簡體字	手 寫	筆 順
味	味	味	味味 味味 味味 味 味

甲骨文	金 文	小 篆
		𣢟

🔔 舌頭品嘗東西得到的感覺：the sensation conveyed by the tongue in contact with food

五味：酸、甜、苦、辣、鹹：five tastes— sour, sweet, bitter, spicy, salty

🔔 鼻子聞東西得到的感覺：odors sensed by the nose

香味：fragrance

🔔 菜餚：dish

山珍海味：delicacies from the land and sea

4/26 七 | 拼音 | qī | ㄑㄧ

正體字	簡體字	手 寫	筆 順
七	七	七	七 七

甲骨文	金 文	小 篆
	十	㐅

🔔 數量詞「七」：the number seven

七件衣服：seven pieces of clothes

🔔 次序排第七的：七 can also be used as an ordinal number, the seventh.

第七號：the seventh

> 七是個幸運數字。
> "7" is a lucky number.

4 27 合

| 拼音 | hé | ㄏㄜˊ |

正體字	簡體字	手 寫	筆 順
合	合	合	合合合合合

甲骨文	金 文	小 篆

※ 關閉、合攏：to close or to shut

　合不攏嘴：to grin from ear to ear

※ 聚集：to gather

　集合：to assemble

※ 相符：in accordance with

　合法：legal

　合作：to cooperate

由於合作促進我們企業的成長。
Cooperation spurred our company to grow.

4 28 拾

| 拼音 | shí | ㄕˊ |

正體字	簡體字	手 寫	筆 順
拾	拾	拾	拾拾拾拾拾

甲骨文	金 文	小 篆
		拾

※ 撿取、拿起： to pick up

　拾金不昧：to return to the owner what one finds

※ 收集、收斂、整理： to collect, arrange

　收拾：to tidy up

請把房間收拾乾淨。
Please tidy up the room.

※ 數字十的意思：ten

④29 又 拼音 yòu ㄧ ㄡˋ

正體字	簡體字	手 寫	筆 順
又	又	又	又 又

甲骨文	金 文	小 篆
ㄟ	ㄋ	ㄋ

🔔 表示「重複的動作」：repeated actions

　看了又看：to look again and again

🔔 表示更加強一層：to emphasize

> 他的病又加重了。
> The patient's condition is getting worse.

🔔 表示附加的數目：additional numbers

　一又二分之一：one and a half

④30 叉 拼音 chā ㄔㄚ

正體字	簡體字	手 寫	筆 順
叉	叉	叉	又 又 叉

甲骨文	金 文	小 篆
ㄟ	ㄋ	ㄋ

🔔 手指交錯：crossed fingers

　交叉：to cross, to intersect

🔔 一端有分歧的器物：a split or fray in one
　end of an object

　叉子：fork

　刀叉：knife and fork

> 我不習慣用刀叉吃飯。
> I am not used to using knives and forks.

🔔 分歧的：difference, divergence

　叉路：a fork in a road

5月
May

5/1 止 拼音 zhǐ ㄓˇ

正體字	簡體字	手寫
止	止	止

甲骨文	金文	小篆
止	止	止

筆順
止
止
止
止

禁止：to prohibit, ban

停止：stop

> 請停止說話。
> Please stop talking.

> 校園內禁止吸菸。
> Smoking is prohibited on school grounds.

使……停住：to make something stop

止痛：stop pain

5/2 正 拼音 zhèng ㄓㄥˋ

正體字	簡體字	手寫
正	正	正

甲骨文	金文	小篆
正	正	正

筆順
正
正
正
正
正

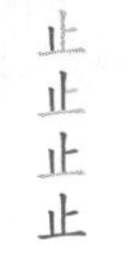

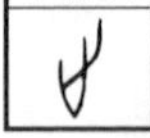

不偏斜的：not leaning, impartial

正午：noon

表示動作正在進行的狀態：「正」 means the action of moving.

正在：in the process of

> 外面正在下雨。
> It is raining outside.

修改錯誤：to revise, alter

訂正：to make corrections

5/3 東 拼音 dōng ㄉㄨㄥ

正體字	簡體字	手寫
東	东	東

筆 順
東 東 東 東 東 東 東 東

甲骨文	金 文	小 篆
✡	✡	東

☼ 日出的方向：the direction in which the sun rises

東方：east

太陽從東方出來。
The sun rises in the east.

東歐：Eastern Europe

☼ 物品：thing, stuff

東西：thing

我把東西交由火車運走。
I sent my stuff by train.

5/4 西 拼音 xī ㄒㄧ

正體字	簡體字	手寫
西	西	西

筆 順
西 西 西 西 西 西 西 西 西

甲骨文	金 文	小 篆
⊕	⊗	西

☼ 方位名。為日落的一方，與東相對：the direction in which the sun sets, the opposite of east

由西往東：from west to east

☼ 西邊的：west

日落西山。
The sun is setting in the west.

☼ 西方、歐美國家的：western or European countries

西餐：western-style food

5/5 立 拼音 lì ㄌㄧˋ

正體字	簡體字	手寫	筆順
立	立	立	立 立 立 立 立

甲骨文	金文	小篆
𡗥	𡗥	𡗥

🔔 站立：to stand up

立正：to stand straight

> 大家立正站好。
> Stand at attention.

🔔 制定、訂定：「立」can also mean to establish, draw up.

立法：to legislate, to make laws

立法院：the Legislative Yuan

立法委員：legislator

🔔 立刻：at once

5/6 占 拼音 zhān ㄓㄢ

正體字	簡體字	手寫	筆順
占	占	占	占 占 占 占 占

甲骨文	金文	小篆
𠧞		占

🔔 用說話來解釋占卜的結果，以推測吉凶：
to explain the results of divination and predict whether one will have good or bad fortune

占卜：to practice divination; divine

> 吉普賽人用水晶球來占卜。
> Gypsies use crystall balls to augur well (ill).

🔔 據有：「占」when pronounced zhàn (ㄓㄢˋ), it can also mean to occupy.

占據：to occupy

5/7 站 拼音 zhàn ㄓㄢ

正體字	簡體字	手寫	筆順
站	站	站	站站 站站 站站 站站 站站

甲骨文	金文	小篆	

直立：upright

站姿：stance

他的站姿很英挺。
He stands tall and straight.

旅途中供人休息或轉換交通工具的地方：
a place for people to rest or change vehicles

車站：a station

場所或地點：place or place

加油站：gas station

5/8 佔 拼音 zhàn ㄓㄢ

正體字	簡體字	手寫	筆順
佔	占	佔	佔佔 佔佔 佔 佔 佔

甲骨文	金文	小篆	

強力奪取、佔為己有：「佔」means taking something by force and keeping it for yourself.

侵佔：to invade and occupy

侵佔別人的物品是違法的行為。
It is illegal to seize others' goods.

佔領：to capture, to seize

⑤9 店　拼音　diàn　ㄉㄧㄢˋ

正體字	簡體字	手寫	筆順
店	店	店	店 店 店 店 店 店 店 店 店

甲骨文	金文	小篆

🔔 販售貨品的地方：a place where goods are sold

　商店：a shop

　書店：a bookstore

> 我是這家書店的老主顧。
> I am a regular customer at this bookstore.

　商店街：shopping street

🔔 商店的員工：people who work in shops

　店員：shop assistant

⑤10 乙　拼音　yǐ　ㄧˇ

正體字	簡體字	手寫	筆順
乙	乙	乙	乙

甲骨文	金文	小篆
↘	↘	↘

🔔 排序第二，同 A、B、C、D……排序的 B：In English, A, B, C, D... are used to indicate rank or order. In Chinese, we use 甲, 乙, 丙, 丁...

　乙等：level 2

> 他這次的數學成績是乙等。
> Hi got a "B" on his math task.

　乙班：the second class

5/11 食　拼音　shí　ㄕˊ

正體字	簡體字	手 寫	筆 順
食	食	食	食 食 食 食 食 食 食 食 食

甲骨文	金 文	小 篆
𩙿	𩚛	𩙿

🔔 吃的東西：「食」refers to the things you eat.

食物：food

> 中國食物很好吃。
> Chinese food is delicious.

🔔 吃飯：to have a meal

進食：to take food

🔔 嘗到、承受：to taste, bear

自食惡果：be hoisted by one's own petard; become the victim of one's own evil deeds

5/12 包　拼音　bāo　ㄅㄠ

正體字	簡體字	手 寫	筆 順
包	包	包	包 包 包 包

甲骨文	金 文	小 篆
		𠣬

🔔 用紙或布等東西把物品包起來：to wrap something in paper or cloth

包裝：to package, to wrap

🔔 裝東西的袋子：a bag, a briefcase

皮包：handbag, briefcase

後背包：backpack

> 他揹著一個很重的後背包。
> He had a heavey backpack on his back.

🔔 包子：steamed stuffed bun

5/13 飽 拼音 bǎo ㄅㄠ

正體字	簡體字	手寫	筆順
飽	饱	飽	飽飽飽 飽飽飽 飽飽飽 飽飽 飽飽

甲骨文	金文	小篆
		飽

🔔 **吃飽**：to eat till full

我吃飽了。
I'm full.

🔔 充足、充分：adequate, abundant
飽和：saturation

5/14 抱 拼音 bào ㄅㄠ

正體字	簡體字	手寫	筆順
抱	抱	抱	抱抱 抱抱 抱抱 抱

甲骨文	金文	小篆
		抱

🔔 用手臂圍住：to hold with both arms
擁抱：to embrace, to hug

我擁抱好久不見的朋友。
I hug friends who I haven't seen in a long time.

🔔 志向、理想：aspiration, ideal
抱負：aspiration, ambition

🔔 懷藏在內：to keep inside
抱怨：to complain

⑤ 15 足　拼音　zú　ㄗㄨˊ

正體字	簡體字	手寫	筆順
足	足	足	足 足 足 足 足 足 足

甲骨文	金文	小篆
足	足	足

🔔 人體下肢的總稱。也稱為「腳」：foot

足跡：footprint

🔔 夠量的、不缺乏的：sufficient

足夠：enough, sufficient

🔔 值得：worth

心滿意足：perfectly contented

孩子的成就，令母親心滿意足。
The child's achievement satisfied his mother.

⑤ 16 各　拼音　gè　ㄍㄜˋ

正體字	簡體字	手寫	筆順
各	各	各	各 各 各 各 各 各 各

甲骨文	金文	小篆
各	各	各

🔔 代替一定群體中的不同個體本身：each, every

各自：each

我們各自從家裡出發。
We each set out from our homes.

各人自掃門前雪。
Let every man skin his own skunk.

🔔 每：each

各個：every

⑤17 路 　拼音　lù　　ㄌㄨˋ

正體字	簡體字	手　寫
路	路	路

甲骨文	金　文	小　篆
	路	路

筆　順
路路路
路路路
路路路
路路
路路

🔔 給人、車走的途徑：a way/road/path for people or vehicles

道路：road

高速公路：freeway

假日的高速公路經常塞車。
The highway is often packed on holidays.

⑤18 跑 　拼音　pǎo　　ㄆㄠˇ

正體字	簡體字	手　寫
跑	跑	跑

甲骨文	金　文	小　篆

筆　順
跑跑跑
跑跑跑
跑跑
跑跑
跑跑

🔔 快走：to walk fast

跑步：to run

下班後，我有跑步運動的習慣。
I go running after work.

🔔 逃走、躲避：to run away, to avoid

逃跑：to escape

跑掉：to run away

5/19 泡 拼音 pào ㄆ ㄠˋ

正體字	簡體字	手寫	筆順
泡	泡	泡	泡 泡 泡 泡 泡 泡 泡

甲骨文	金文	小篆
		泡

🔔 在水面上漂浮，內含氣體的球狀物：ball shaped objects that float on water

水泡：bubble

🔔 泡狀的物體：an object shaped like a bubble

燈泡：light bulb

🔔 用水沖浸：to pour water on...

泡茶：to make tea

5/20 及 拼音 jí ㄐ ㄧˊ

正體字	簡體字	手寫	筆順
及	及	及	及 及 及 及

甲骨文	金文	小篆
𠬝	𠬝	及

🔔 追上：to catch up

及時：in time

還好我及時趕到。
Fortunately, I made it in time.

及時相助的朋友才是真朋友。
A friend in need is a friend indeed.

🔔 牽涉：be involved

波及：be affected

🔔 到達：to reach, to arrive

及格：to pass (the exam)

5/21 由 拼音 yóu ㄧㄡˊ

正體字	簡體字	手寫	筆 順
由	由	由	由 由 由 由 由

甲骨文	金 文	小 篆
㞕	㞕	由

- 原因：reason
  - 理由：reason
- 由於：because of
- 從：from
  - 由貧致富：from rags to riches
- 屬於：to come under the authority of

> 這件案子由我負責。
> I am in charge of this case.

5/22 油 拼音 yóu ㄧㄡˊ

正體字	簡體字	手寫	筆 順
油	油	油	油 油 油 油 油 油 油

甲骨文	金 文	小 篆
	㳄	油

- 動物的脂肪，或是從植物、礦物提煉出來的脂狀物：fat, oil
  - 牛油：butter
  - 石油：oil
  - 汽油：gasoline

> 最近國際石油又漲價了。
> The price of oil increased again recently.

- 不實際的言詞：glib
  - 油腔滑調：glib-tongued

5/23 川 拼音 chuān ㄔㄨㄢ

正體字	簡體字	手寫	筆順
川	川	川	川 川 川

甲骨文	金文	小篆
〵〵	〵〵	川

🔔 河流：river

河川：stream; river

> 這條河川潔淨清澈。
> This river is clean and limpid.

🔔 一種烹飪的方法。將食物置於開水中，水一開即刻撈起：to blanch (a cooking method)

川肉片：to blanch sliced meat, 通「汆」(cuān ㄘㄨㄢ)

5/24 八 拼音 bā ㄅㄚ

正體字	簡體字	手寫	筆順
八	八	八	八 八

甲骨文	金文	小篆
八	八	八

🔔 數量詞「八」：the number eight

八雙鞋子：eight pairs of shoes

> 他買八雙鞋子送給八個人。
> He bought eight pairs of shoes and gave them to eight people.

🔔 次序排第八：「八」can also be used as an ordinal number, the eighth.

第八名：eighth prize

⑤25 年　拼音　nián　ㄋㄧㄢˊ

正體字	簡體字	手　寫
年	年	年

甲骨文	金　文	小　篆
𥞉	𥞉	秊

筆　順
年
年
年
年
年

🔔 農作物收成：crop; harvest

　　豐年：good harvest

🔔 時間的單位：「年」is also used as a measure of time.

　　一年：a year

> 一年有四季：春、夏、秋、冬。
> There are four seasons in a year—spring, summer, autumn and winter.

⑤26 光　拼音　guāng　ㄍㄨㄤ

正體字	簡體字	手　寫
光	光	光

甲骨文	金　文	小　篆
𤇾	𤇾	光

筆　順
光
光
光
光
光

🔔 光線：light, ray

　　日光：sunlight

　　燈光：lamp light

🔔 時間：time

　　時光：time

🔔 用完：to be used up

　　用光：to be used up

⑤27 名 　拼音　míng　ㄇㄧㄥˊ

正體字	簡體字	手　寫	筆　順
名	名	名	名名名名名

甲骨文	金　文	小　篆
𠙾	召	名

🔔 人或事物的稱謂：the title of a person or an object

　名字：name

> 「臺北」是一個地名。
> Taipei is a place name.

🔔 有名：famous

🔔 地名：place name

🔔 聲譽：reputation

　盛名：great reputation

　名不虛傳：One's fame is indeed deserved.

⑤28 民 　拼音　mín　ㄇㄧㄣˊ

正體字	簡體字	手　寫	筆　順
民	民	民	民民民民民

甲骨文	金　文	小　篆
	𫩏	民

🔔 社會的基本成員：members of a society

　人民：the people

> 生活在這裡的人民都很快樂長壽。
> People here all lead long and happy lives.

　公民：citizen

🔔 人或人群：a human or a group of humans

　民族：ethic group

　居民：resident

🔔 民主：democracy

⑤/29 去 拼音 qù ㄑㄩˋ

正體字	簡體字	手 寫	筆 順
去	去	去	去去去去去

甲骨文	金 文	小 篆

🔔 往、到。與「來」相對：to go, arrive

「去」is the opposite of "come".

出去：to go out

🔔 死亡：to die, death

去世：to pass away

🔔 過去的：past

去年：last year

> 他父親在去年去世了。
> His father passed away last year.

⑤/30 法 拼音 fǎ ㄈㄚˇ

正體字	簡體字	手 寫	筆 順
法	法	法	法法法法法法法法

甲骨文	金 文	小 篆
		灋

📖 字的形狀像是古代的神獸，負責審理有罪的案件，進行審判：「法」resembles the miraculous beast in ancient China whose responsibility is to try the guilty.

🔔 **法律**：the law

> 遵守法律是公民的基本素養。
> Obeying the law is a basic requirement of any citizen.

🔔 處理事物的手段：means, method, ways

方法：method

⑤31 生　拼音　shēng　ㄕㄥ

正體字	簡體字	手　寫	筆　順
生	生	生	生 生 生 生

甲骨文	金　文	小　篆
￥	￥	￥

✎ 長出、生長：to send forth, grow

　　產生：to arise, to produce

✎ 學習者：learner

　　學生：student

> 他是一位好學生。
> He is a good student.

✎ 沒有煮熟的：raw

　　生肉：raw meat, raw fish

*6*月
June

6/1 姓 拼音 xìng ㄒㄧㄥˋ

正體字	簡體字	手寫
姓	姓	姓

甲骨文	金文	小篆

筆順
姓姓 姓姓 姓姓 姓 姓

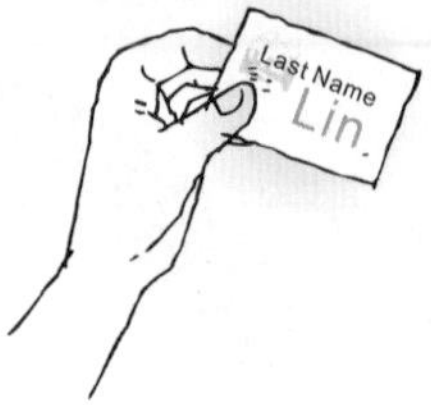

表示個人所屬家族及區別家族的符號：「姓」represents family name.

姓氏：surname

姓名：surname and given name

> 這張名片上印有我的姓名。
> This business card has my name on it.

6/2 克 拼音 kè ㄎㄜˋ

正體字	簡體字	手寫
克	克	克

甲骨文	金文	小篆

筆順
克克 克克 克 克 克

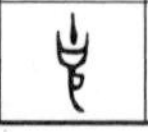

制服、約束：to restrict

克服：to conquer

> 我能夠克服困難，達成目標。
> I can overcome the difficulties and achieve the goal.

計算重量的單位：a unit of weight

一公克：a gram

6/3 同 拼音 tóng ㄊㄨㄥˊ

正體字	簡體字	手 寫	筆 順
同	同	同	同同同同同同

甲骨文	金 文	小 篆
𠔸	㕥	同

✎ 會合：to join, to meet

會同：to handle an affair jointly with other concerned organizations

✎ 一樣：same

相同：the same, alike

> 我和他有相同的嗜好。
> I have the same hobbies as him.

✎ 契約：contract, agreement

合同：agreement, contract

6/4 旦 拼音 dàn ㄉㄢˋ

正體字	簡體字	手 寫	筆 順
旦	旦	旦	旦旦旦旦旦

甲骨文	金 文	小 篆
日	旦	旦

📖 旦的意思就是太陽剛從地平線升上來：

「旦」indicates the rising sun just above the horizon.

✎ 天剛亮的時候：daybreak

通宵達旦：all through the night

> 大家通宵達旦的開宴會。
> Everyone sang and danced all through the night at the party.

✎ 一年的第一天：the first date of the year

元旦：New Year's Day

⑥/5 但 　拼音　 dàn 　ㄉㄢ

正體字	簡體字	手寫	筆　順
但	但	但	但 但 但 但 但 但 但 但

甲骨文	金 文	小 篆
		但

🔔 僅、只：only, merely, barely
　　但願：if only

🔔 儘管：feel free to..., although
　　但說無妨：There's no harm in saying what one thinks.

🔔 不過、可是：but, however

> 你可以去玩，但是要先做完功課。
> You can go out and play but you have to finish your homework first.

⑥/6 走 　拼音　 zǒu 　ㄗㄡˇ

正體字	簡體字	手寫	筆　順
走	走	走	走 走 走 走 走 走 走

甲骨文	金 文	小 篆
大	走	走

🔔 前進：to go forward, march
　　走路：to walk

> 我喜歡走路上班。
> I like to go to work on foot.

🔔 離開：to leave
　　走開：to go away, walk away

🔔 供行走的道路：a foot path
　　走道：pavement, sidewalk, footpath, aisle

正體字	簡體字	手 寫	筆 順
角	角	角	角 角 角 角 角

甲骨文	金 文	小 篆

動物頭上的角：horn

牛角：ox horn

角落：corner

> 角落裡有蟲。
> There are bugs in the corner.

競爭、較量：to compete, to race

口角：to argue

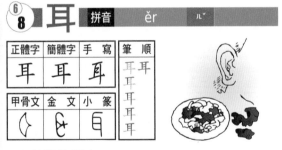

正體字	簡體字	手 寫	筆 順
耳	耳	耳	耳 耳 耳 耳 耳

甲骨文	金 文	小 篆

聽覺的器官：organ of hearing

外耳：external ear

聽說：to have heard

耳聞：to have heard of

> 耳聞不如目見。
> Seeing for oneself is better than hearing from others.

6/9 見 拼音 jiàn ㄐㄧㄢˋ

正體字	簡體字	手寫	筆順
見	见	見	見見見見見見見見

甲骨文	金文	小篆

🔔 看到：to see
　　看見：to catch sight of
🔔 表示一個人的看法：perspective, point of view
　　遠見：foresight

> 他是一位很有遠見的領導者。
> He is a leader with foresight.

　　偏見：prejudice
🔔 接待：to welcome, to receive
　　接見：to receive somebody

6/10 元 拼音 yuán ㄩㄢˊ

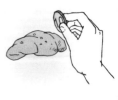

正體字	簡體字	手寫	筆順
元	元	元	元元元元

甲骨文	金文	小篆

🔔 開始的、第一的：primary, first
　　元旦：the New Year's Day
🔔 單位量詞：a unit of money
　　十元：ten dollars

> 我買了一個十元的麵包。
> I bought a loaf of bread which cost me ten dollars.

🔔 帶領的人：leader
　　元首：head of a state

6/11 用 　拼音　yòng　ㄩㄥˋ

正體字	簡體字	手　寫	筆　順
用	用	用	用 用 用 用 用

甲骨文	金　文	小　篆	
爿	肖	用	

🔔 可以施行：usable

　　使用：to use

🔔 功能、效果：function, effect

　　功用：function

🔔 花費的錢財：expense

　　費用：expense

> 這次聚餐的費用，大家平均分擔。
> We split the cost of dinner.

6/12 只 　拼音　zhǐ　ㄓˇ

正體字	簡體字	手　寫	筆　順
只	只	只	只 只 只 只

甲骨文	金　文	小　篆	
	只	只	

🔔 但是：只 means but.

　　只是：only, merely

🔔 僅僅：only, merely, barely, just

　　只能：only, to have no other choice

> 他牙疼，只能吃流質食物。
> He can only have liquid food because of
> his toothache.

6/13 定 拼音 dìng ㄉㄧㄥˋ

正體字	簡體字	手寫	筆順
定	定	定	定定定定定定定定

甲骨文	金文	小篆
	俞	鼎

🔔 平靜：calm, stable

　　安定：stable, settled

🔔 確切：definite, exact

　　一定：surely, certainly

🔔 使確定、不更改：make sure, not change

　　決定：to decide

性格決定命運。
One's personality determines one's destiny.

6/14 平 拼音 píng ㄆㄧㄥˊ

正體字	簡體字	手寫	筆順
平	平	平	平平平平平

甲骨文	金文	小篆
	平	平

🔔 不突出的：not projecting out

　　平地：flat ground

🔔 一般的、普通的：common

　　平民：the common people

🔔 均等的：fair, equal

　　平均：even, average

🔔 和平：peace

追求和平是我們共同的期望。
Our common hope is to seek peace.

6/15 衣　拼音　yī　一

正體字	簡體字	手　寫	筆　順
衣	衣	衣	衣衣衣衣衣衣

甲骨文	金　文	小　篆
仒	仒	仒

:::: 穿在身上，可以蔽體的東西。：clothes

毛衣：woolen sweater

> 我買了一件紅色的毛衣。
> I bought a red woolen sweater.

:::: 包在東西外面的保護層：be coated with

糖衣：sugar coat

:::: 指苔蘚類，附著在岩石上的植物：moss or other plants that grow on rocks

苔衣、地衣：lichen

6/16 牙　拼音　yá　ㄧㄚˊ

正體字	簡體字	手　寫	筆　順
牙	牙	牙	牙牙牙牙

甲骨文	金　文	小　篆
	丂	丂

:::: 口腔裡用來咀嚼、磨碎食物的器官：tooth

牙齒：tooth

門牙：front teeth

牙刷：toothbrush

牙籤：toothpick

牙科醫師：dentist

> 我的牙齒很健全。
> All my teeth are good.

6/17 身 拼音 shēn ㄕㄣ

正體字	簡體字	手 寫	筆 順
身	身	身	身身身身身身

甲骨文	金 文	小 篆

☆ 是人或動物的軀體：「身」means the body of a human or animal.

　身體：body

☆ 物體的中心或主要部分：the center or main part of an object

　船身：the body of a ship

☆ 地位：position

　身分：position

> 我目前的身分是老師。
> My present occupation is a teacher.

6/18 古 拼音 gǔ ㄍㄨˇ

正體字	簡體字	手 寫	筆 順
古	古	古	古古古古古

甲骨文	金 文	小 篆

☆ 過去久遠的時代：remote era in the past

　古代：ancient

> 他是研究古代歷史的學者。
> He is a scholar who studies ancient history.

☆ 過去的、舊的：in the past; old

　古人：the ancients

☆ 姓氏：a surname

正體字	簡體字	手 寫	筆 順
吉	吉	吉	吉 吉 吉 吉 吉 吉

甲骨文	金 文	小 篆
𠮷	吉	吉

好：good

吉利：lucky

過新年說吉祥話。
Say auspicious things during the New Year season.

有利的事：something that is beneficial

趨吉避凶：to pursue luck and avoid disaster

正體字	簡體字	手 寫	筆 順
失	失	失	失 失 失 失 失

甲骨文	金 文	小 篆
		失

丟掉、遺落：to lose; to leave something behind

遺失：lose

我在車站遺失了皮包。
I lost a handbag in the station.

違背：go against

失禮：impoliteness

錯誤：mistake

過失：fault; mistake

失敗者：loser

6/21 朱

拼音	zhū	ㄓㄨ

正體字	簡體字	手寫
朱	朱	朱

甲骨文	金文	小篆
朱	朱	朱

筆順：朱 朱 朱 朱 朱

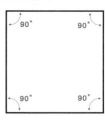

🔔 紅色：red
　　朱紅：bright red
🔔 姓氏：a surname

朱先生種了許多朱紅色的花。
Mr. Zhu has planted a lot of bright red flowers.

6/22 方

拼音	fāng	ㄈㄤ

正體字	簡體字	手寫
方	方	方

甲骨文	金文	小篆
方	方	方

筆順：方 方 方 方

🔔 四個角都是九十度的四邊形：a quadrilateral with four 90° angles
　　正方形：square
　　長方形：rectangle
🔔 辦法：method, way
　　方法：method, means
　　方式：way

解決問題要有適當的方法。
Problems should be solved using appropriate means.

6/23 公 拼音 gōng ㄍㄨㄥ

正體字	簡體字	手寫	筆順
公	公	公	公 公 公 公
甲骨文	金文	小篆	

- 以平分物品來表示公平：to divide equally
  - **公平**：fair

    他為人公平正直。
    He is a fair-minded man.
- 使多數人得知或分享：to share with others
  - **公布**：to publish, to announce
- 雄性的：male
  - **公雞**：a rooster
  - **公羊**：ram

6/24 少 拼音 shǎo ㄕㄠˇ

正體字	簡體字	手寫	筆順
少	少	少	少 少 少 少
甲骨文	金文	小篆	

- 不多：not much
  - **很少**：few
  - **少數**：minority

    我用很少的錢買不少的東西。
    I bought a lot of things with very little money.
- 不夠：not enough
  - **缺少**：lack, shortage of
- 年輕的：young
  - **少年**：juvenile

⑥ 25 妙 拼音 miào ㄇㄧㄠˋ

正體字	簡體字	手 寫	筆 順
妙	妙	妙	妙妙 妙妙 妙妙 妙 妙

甲骨文	金 文	小 篆

🔔 美好：nice, good

　美妙：wonderful, great

🔔 神奇、奇巧：m i r a c u l o u s, m a g i c a l, ingenious

　奇妙：wonderful

🔔 有趣的：interesting

　巧妙：ingenious, clever

> 這個點子真妙！
> This is a great/clever idea!

⑥ 26 欠 拼音 qiàn ㄑㄧㄢˋ

正體字	簡體字	手 寫	筆 順
欠	欠	欠	欠 欠 欠 欠

甲骨文	金 文	小 篆
𠘧		𣏃

🔔 張口呵氣：「欠」is breath out with the mouth.

　打呵欠：to yawn

🔔 借人財物未還：to borrow something from someone and not return it. It can also mean to not give something to someone when you should.

　欠錢：to owe someone money

🔔 不夠、缺乏：not enough, be short of, lack

　欠妥：improper

6/27 有 　拼音　　yǒu　　ㄧㄡˇ

正體字	簡體字	手寫	筆順
有	有	有	有 有 有 有 有

甲骨文	金文	小篆

持有：to have

擁有：to have

> 我擁有兩張銀行的信用卡。
> I have two credit cards.

富有：rich

不確定：uncertain, indeterminate

有一天：someday

有始有終：to carry things through

有其父必有其子：Like father, like son.

6/28 米 　拼音　　mǐ　　ㄇㄧˇ

正體字	簡體字	手寫	筆順
米	米	米	米 米 米 米 米

甲骨文	金文	小篆

📖 字像一些散開的米粒。中間的一條線，表示放置稻米的架子的間隔米：「米」resembles scattered grains. The line in the middle represents a rack with grain on it.

東方人的主食：a staple food in Asia

白米：white rice

計算長度的單位，一米：a unit of length, 1 meter

一米：one meter

⑥29 果 拼音 guǒ ㄍㄨㄛˇ

正體字	簡體字	手寫	筆順
果	果	果	果 果 果 果 果 果 果

甲骨文	金文	小篆
𣎴	果	果

🔔 樹木所結的果實：fruits of trees

　　水果：fruits

> 蘋果是我最喜歡吃的水果。
> Apples are one of my favorite fruits.

🔔 事情的成效或結局：the effect or result of something

　　成果：achievement

🔔 事情和所預料的一樣：things happen as expected

　　果然：as expected

⑥30 交 拼音 jiāo ㄐㄧㄠ

正體字	簡體字	手寫	筆順
交	交	交	交 交 交 交 交 交 交

甲骨文	金文	小篆
交	交	交

🔔 相交：to cross

　　交錯：to intertwine

🔔 好朋友：good friends

　　至交：a very close friend

🔔 買賣：dealings, transactions

　　成交：to make a deal

> 這筆買賣就這樣成交了。
> The deal is clinched.

🔔 交通工具：mode of transportation

7月
July

⑴1 告　拼音　gào　《ㄠˋ

正體字	簡體字	手 寫	筆 順
告	告	告	告告 告告 告 告

甲骨文	金 文	小 篆
⅏	⅏	𠮷

🔔 訴說、報告：to tell, to report

　告訴：to tell

> 他被告知得到大獎。
> He was told that he had won a big prize.

🔔 揭發、提出訴訟：to disclose, to take legal action

　控告：to appeal

🔔 對大眾宣布的語言或文字：words used in an announcement

　廣告：the advertisement

⑴2 勾　拼音　gōu　《ㄡ

正體字	簡體字	手 寫	筆 順
勾	勾	勾	勾 勾 勾 勾

甲骨文	金 文	小 篆

🔔 勾著：hook

　勾住：catch; hang

> 這人用拐杖勾住路燈。
> The man hooked the street lamp with his cane.

🔔 暗地相通：communicate secretly

　勾結：to collude with; collusion

> 官商勾結是犯法的。
> It is illegal for people in government to collude with people in business.

3 世 拼音 shì ㄕˋ

正體字	簡體字	手 寫	筆 順
世	世	世	世世世世世

甲骨文	金 文	小 篆
	世	世

🔔 一輩子：one's whole life
　一生一世：one's whole life

你是我這一生一世最愛的人。
You are the love of my life.

🔔 人間：human world, the world
　世界：world

🔔 計算年代的單位：a time unit
　世紀：century

4 兄 拼音 xiōng ㄒㄩㄥ

正體字	簡體字	手 寫	筆 順
兄	兄	兄	兄兄兄兄兄

甲骨文	金 文	小 篆
ヷ	界	界

🔔 哥哥：elder brother
　兄長：elder brother
　長兄：eldest brother

中國人常說長兄如父。
The Chinese often regard the eldest brother as father.

🔔 朋友間相互的敬稱：a respectful title between friends
　仁兄：dear friend

7 / 5 弟

| 拼音 | dì | ㄉ一ˋ |

正體字	簡體字	手 寫	筆 順
弟	弟	弟	弟弟 弟弟 弟弟 弟弟 弟

甲骨文	金 文	小 篆

☆ 弟弟：younger brother

　 小弟：little brother

> 小弟是個感情豐富的孩子。
> My little brother is a sentimental boy.

☆ 門徒、學生：follower, student

　 弟子：disciple

> 孔子有72弟子。
> Confucius had 72 disciples.

7 / 6 住

| 拼音 | zhù | ㄓㄨˋ |

正體字	簡體字	手 寫	筆 順
住	住	住	住住 住住 住 住 住

甲骨文	金 文	小 篆

☆ 長期居留：to stay for a long time

　 居住：to reside

> 他長期居住在國外。
> He lives abroad most of the time.

☆ 停止：to stop

　 住手：to stop

　 住口：stop talking

☆ 表示停頓、靜止：be still

　 站住：to freeze

　 坐不住：cannot sit still

7/7 往　拼音　wǎng　ㄨㄤˇ

正體字	簡體字	手　寫	筆　順
往	往	往	往往往往往往往往

甲骨文	金　文	小　篆
	徃	徃

◌ 去、到：to go to

　前往：to go to

> 我們正要前往百貨公司。
> We are about to go to the department store.

◌ 朝向某個方向：towards

　往東走：towards the east

◌ 交朋友：make friends

　交往：associate with

7/8 反　拼音　fǎn　ㄈㄢˇ

正體字	簡體字	手　寫	筆　順
反	反	反	反反反反

甲骨文	金　文	小　篆
	反	冃

大

小

◌ 與「正」相反：the opposite of「正」

　反面：back, reverse side

　反敗為勝：to turn the tide

　反義：antonym

> 「熱」是「冷」的反義詞。
> "Hot" is an antonym of "cold".

◌ 不贊成：to disagree

　反對：object to

> 這件事情我持反對的看法。
> I have opposing opinions in this issue.

⑦ 9 飯

| 拼音 | fàn | ㄈㄢˋ |

正體字	簡體字	手 寫	筆 順
飯	饭	飯	飯飯飯 飯飯飯 飯飯 飯飯 飯飯

甲骨文	金 文	小 篆
	𩙿	飯

🔔 煮熟的穀類食品：cooked cereal
   米飯：rice

🔔 每天定時吃的正餐：the regular daily meals
   早飯：breakfast
   晚飯：dinner

我習慣用蔬果當作晚餐。
I am used to having vegetables and fruits for dinner.

⑦ 10 幸

| 拼音 | xìng | ㄒㄧㄥˋ |

正體字	簡體字	手 寫	筆 順
幸	幸	幸	幸幸 幸幸 幸幸 幸幸 幸

甲骨文	金 文	小 篆
	𡕒	幸

🔔 高興：happy
   慶幸：rejoice

🔔 好運氣：good luck
   幸運：lucky, good fortune

享受美食真幸福。
It is a blessing to enjoy good food.

🔔 榮耀：glory
   榮幸：honor

認識你是我最大的榮幸。
It is my great honor to know you.

⑦ 11 辛

| 拼音 | xīn | ㄒㄧㄣ |

正體字	簡體字	手寫	筆順
辛	辛	辛	辛 辛 辛 辛 辛 辛 辛

甲骨文	金文	小篆

⎰ 辣的味道：spicy flavour

辛辣：pungent

⎰ 勞苦、勞累：tired, exhausted

辛苦：to work hard

> 我辛苦的工作是為了養家。
> I work hard to support the family.

⎰ 姓氏：a surname

⑦ 12 門

| 拼音 | mén | ㄇㄣˊ |

正體字	簡體字	手寫	筆順
門	门	門	門 門 門 門 門 門 門 門

甲骨文	金文	小篆

⎰ 能關閉出入口的裝置：a door, gate

車門：car door

房門：a door to the house

門票：entrance ticket

門牌：house number

門鈴：the doorbell

門神：door god

> 我用鑰匙打開房門。
> I opened the door with a key.

⑦ 13 問 | 拼音 wèn ㄨㄣˋ

正體字	簡體字	手寫
問	问	問

甲骨文	金文	小篆
𠳐		問

筆順

問 問 問
問 問 問
問 問 問
問 問 問
問 問

🔔 向人請教：to consult

　　詢問、請問：to inquire about

　　詢問處：information desk

🔔 表示關切而探望、拜訪：to pay a visit to show concern

　　問候：to send a greeting

> 請幫我問候令尊。
> Please say hello to your father for me.

🔔 責備、追究：to blame, to investigate

　　追問：make a detailed inquiry

⑦ 14 間 | 拼音 jiàn ㄐㄧㄢˋ

正體字	簡體字	手寫
間	间	間

甲骨文	金文	小篆

筆順

間 間 間
間 間 間
間 間 間
間 間 間
間 間

🔔 空隙：gap

　　間隙：gap

🔔 兩者之間：in between (pronounced jiān ㄐㄧㄢ)

　　中間：in between

🔔 時候：time (pronounced jiān ㄐㄧㄢ)

　　時間：time

> 時間不早了，該睡覺了。
> It is late. You should get to bed.

⑦15 閒　拼音　xián　ㄒㄧㄢˊ

正體字	簡體字	手寫	筆　順
閒	闲	閒	閒 閒 閒 閒 閒 閒 閒 閒 閒 閒 閒 閒 閒 閒
甲骨文	金　文	小　篆	
	門	閒	

💫 空暇無事：to have nothing to do

空閒：leisure

> 他過著閒情逸致的生活。
> He lives his life in a leisurely and carefree manner.

💫 隨意的、不經心的：at will, be casual

閒聊：to chat

> 我們一邊喝咖啡，一邊閒聊文學。
> We had a chat about literature while having coffee.

⑦16 聞　拼音　wén　ㄨㄣˊ

正體字	簡體字	手寫	筆　順
聞	闻	聞	聞 聞 聞 聞 聞 聞 聞 聞 聞 聞 聞 聞 聞 聞
甲骨文	金　文	小　篆	
𦥑		聞	

💫 用鼻子嗅：to sniff

聞到：to smell

💫 音訊、消息：news

新聞：news

> 我常收看電視晚間新聞。
> I often watch evening news on TV.

💫 聽見：to hear

聽聞：to hear about

⑦ 17　閃　拼音　shǎn　ㄕㄢˇ

正體字	簡體字	手 寫	筆 順
閃	闪	閃	閃 閃 閃 閃 閃 閃 閃 閃 閃 閃

甲骨文	金 文	小 篆
		閃

🔔 躲開、躲避：to elude

　　閃躲：to dodge

> 他閃躲狗仔隊的跟蹤。
> He dodged the paparazzi who were following him.

🔔 雷電所發出的光：lightening

　　閃電：lightening

🔔 忽然顯現或搖動不定的：to occur suddenly

　　閃光：flash

⑦ 18　開　拼音　kāi　ㄎㄞ

正體字	簡體字	手 寫	筆 順
開	开	開	開 開 開 開 開 開 開 開 開 開 開 開 開 開

甲骨文	金 文	小 篆
		開

🔔 啟、張：to open

　　開門：to open the door

　　開始：to begin

> 好的開始是成功的一半。
> A good beginning brings you half way to success.

🔔 舒張、綻放：in blossom

　　盛開：blooming, in full flower

🔔 創辦、設立：to establish

　　開店：to set up a shop

⑦ 19 關 拼音 guān ㄍㄨㄢ

正體字	簡體字	手 寫	筆 順
關	关	關	關關關關 關關關關 關關關關 關關關關 關關關關

甲骨文	金 文	小 篆
		關

※ 關閉：to close

關門：to close the door

※ 使作用或功能停止：to cease operating or functioning

關燈：to turn off the light

睡前要關燈。
Turn off the light before going to bed.

※ 事物或時間演進過程中的重要時刻、階段：a critical moment or phase

難關：difficulties, crisis

⑦ 20 求 拼音 qiú ㄑㄧㄡ

正體字	簡體字	手 寫	筆 順
求	求	求	求求 求求 求

甲骨文	金 文	小 篆
求		求

※ 找尋、探索：to search for

請求：to request

※ 拜託：to request somebody to do

求助：to ask for help

如有緊急事件，可打一一〇向警方求助。
Call 110 to ask for help in emergency.

※ 所提出的條件：conditions

要求：requirements

① 21 球

| 拼音 | qiú | ㄑㄧㄡˊ |

正體字	簡體字	手　寫	筆　順
球	球	球	球 球 球 球 球 球 球 球 球 球 球

甲骨文	金　文	小　篆
	球	球

🔔 星球：planet
　　地球：the globe

🔔 球類運動中的器材：balls
　　籃球：basketball
　　棒球：baseball

🔔 量詞，計算球狀物的單位：a measure word

> 我吃了兩球冰淇淋。
> I had two scoops of ice cream.

① 22 青

| 拼音 | qīng | ㄑㄧㄥ |

正體字	簡體字	手　寫	筆　順
青	青	青	青 青 青 青 青 青 青 青

甲骨文	金　文	小　篆
	青	青

🔔 顏色：color
　　青色：green or blue

🔔 藍色的：blue
　　青天白日：the blue sky and bright sun

🔔 年輕：young
　　青春：adolescence, youth

> 青春就該追求夢想。
> Youth is when you should follow your dreams.

⑦/23 清 拼音 qīng ㄑㄧㄥ

正體字	簡體字	手　寫	筆　順
清	清	清	清清清 清清清 清清清 清清清 清清清

甲骨文	金　文	小　篆
		清

🔔 澄澈乾淨的水流：clean and clear water

　清澈：crystal clear

🔔 使事物乾淨、整齊：to make things clean and neat

　清洗：to wash

　清理：to clean

> 他幫忙清洗碗筷。
> He helped wash the dishes.

🔔 結帳：to pay the bill

　付清：to pay off

⑦/24 請 拼音 qǐng ㄑㄧㄥ

正體字	簡體字	手　寫	筆　順
請	请	請	請請請 請請請 請請請 請請請 請請請

甲骨文	金　文	小　篆
	請	請

🔔 懇求、乞求：to request, to beg

　請假：to ask for leave

　請病假：to call in sick

🔔 邀約：to invite

　邀請：to invite

> 他邀請我們去他家用餐。
> He invited us for dinner at his home.

🔔 敬詞：term of esteem honorific

　請教：to consult

⑦25 美 拼音 měi ㄇㄟˇ

正體字	簡體字	手 寫
美	美	美

筆 順
美美 美美 美美 美美 美

甲骨文	金 文	小 篆
𦍌	𦍌	美

📖 字像是一個人，頭上戴著羊角或羽毛的裝飾，打扮得十分美麗：「美」resembles a beautiful person, wearing goat horns and feather as decoration.

🔔 美麗：beautiful

> 她是一位美麗的姑娘。
> She is a pretty girl.

🔔 稱讚別人：to compliment, to praise
　　讚美：to compliment

⑦26 風 拼音 fēng ㄈㄥ

正體字	簡體字	手 寫
風	风	風

筆 順
風風 風風 風風 風風 風

甲骨文	金 文	小 篆
		𩖕

🔔 空氣流動的現象：a kind of air flow

　　微風：breeze

　　颱風：typhoon

> 大風把傘吹壞了。
> A strong wind blew the umbrella inside out.

🔔 景象：scene
　　風景：scenery

🔔 習俗：custom
　　風俗：custom

27 涼

| 拼音 | liáng | ㄌㄧㄤˊ |

正體字	簡體字	手寫	筆順
涼	凉	涼	涼涼涼 涼涼 涼涼 涼涼 涼涼

甲骨文	金文	小篆
		㵾

🔔 冷、微寒：cold, cool

涼風：cool breeze

涼水：cool water

🔔 冷清、不熱鬧：desolate, deserted and quiet, not lively

荒涼：bleak and desolate

那座荒涼的小島人煙稀少。
There are few residents on that bleak and desolate island.

🔔 姓氏：a surname

28 支

| 拼音 | zhī | ㄓ |

正體字	簡體字	手寫	筆順
支	支	支	支 支 支 支

甲骨文	金文	小篆
		㪔

🔔 旁系、分出的派別：collateral line

分支：branch

🔔 量詞，計算的單位：a measuring term, the unit for teams and songs

一支歌曲：a song

兩支隊伍：two teams

🔔 付款：payment

開支：revenue and expenditure

我們必須控制這個月的開支。
We have to control expenses this month.

(1) 29 枝 拼音 zhī ㄓ

正體字	簡體字	手寫	筆順
枝	枝	枝	枝 枝 枝 枝 枝 枝 枝 枝

甲骨文	金文	小篆
		枝

🔔 植物主幹旁生的枝條：branch, twig

　　樹枝：branch

　　枝葉：branches and leaves

🔔 量詞，計算細長物體的單位：a measuring term, a unit for slender objects

　　一枝筆：a pencil

> 請問這一枝筆是誰的？
> May I ask whose pen this is?

(1) 30 技 拼音 jì ㄐㄧ

正體字	簡體字	手寫	筆順
技	技	技	技 技 技 技 技 技 技

甲骨文	金文	小篆
		技

🔔 才藝，專門的本領：talents, expertise

　　演技：acting skills

　　絕技：stunt

> 他精於射箭技藝。
> He is skilled with bow and arrow.

🔔 運用專門技術的能力：skill

　　技能、技巧：skill

> 他鋼琴的技巧十分精湛。
> His piano playing skills are excellent.

⑦ 31 甲 　拼音　jiǎ　ㄐㄧㄚ

正體字	簡體字	手　寫	筆　順
甲	甲	甲	甲 甲 甲 甲 甲

甲骨文	金　文	小　篆
十	十	甲

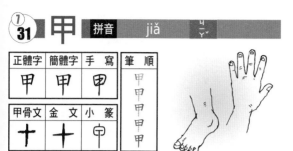

☼ 古代軍人作戰時所穿的衣物：protective equipment soldiers wore in ancient times

　盔甲：armor

☼ 手指、腳指上的角質硬殼：horny plate on tips of fingers and toes

　指甲：nails

> 她的指甲塗上美麗的顏色。
> She painted her finger nails with beautiful colors.

☼ 等地最優秀的：outstanding, excellent

　甲等：grade A

8月
August

8/1 今 拼音 jīn ㄐㄧㄣ

正體字	簡體字	手 寫	筆 順
今	今	今	今今今今

甲骨文	金 文	小 篆

🔔 現在：present, now

> 今天：today

> 今天是我的生日。
> Today is my birthday.

🔔 現代：modern

> 今年：this year

> 古今：in ancient and modern times

> 今非昔比：He is not the man he was.

8/2 令 拼音 lìng ㄌㄧㄥ

正體字	簡體字	手 寫	筆 順
令	令	令	令令令令令

甲骨文	金 文	小 篆
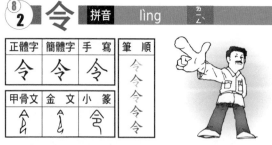		

🔔 發號施令：to give an order

> 命令：order

> 法令：decree

> 軍人須服從命令。
> Soldiers must obey orders.

🔔 敬詞，用來尊稱他人的親屬：honorific title

> 令尊：your father

> 令郎：your son

> 令堂：your mother

8/3 注 拼音 zhù ㄓㄨˋ

正體字	簡體字	手　寫	筆　順
注	注	注	注 注 注 注 注 注 注 注 注

甲骨文	金　文	小　篆
		𣲷

- 灌入：to pour into
  灌注：to pour into
- 心神凝聚集中：focusing on something
  專注：to focus one's attention

  他心神專注地看書。
  He is utterly absorbed in the book.

- 賭博時所下的財物：wager
  賭注：wager; stake

8/4 柱 拼音 zhù ㄓㄨˋ

正體字	簡體字	手　寫	筆　順
柱	柱	柱	柱 柱 柱 柱 柱 柱 柱 柱 柱

甲骨文	金　文	小　篆
		𣝕

- 支撐房屋的柱子：「柱」is the pillar used to support structures.
  樑柱：beam, pillar

  希臘神廟的柱子非常壯觀。
  The pillars of Greek temples are magnificent.

- 形容形狀細長像柱子的東西：「柱」is also used to describe long, thin things.
  水柱：waterspout, water column

8/5 活 拼音 huó ㄏㄨㄛˊ

正體字	簡體字	手　寫	筆　順
活	活	活	活 活 活 活 活 活 活 活 活

甲骨文	金　文	小　篆
		𣴎

🔔 流水聲：the sound of flowing water

🔔 有生命的：living, alive

　活人：a living man

　活力：energy

> 他很有活力。
> He is energetic.

🔔 生動的：vivid

　活潑：lively

> 這個小孩天真活潑又可愛。
> The kid is innocent, energetic, and cute.

8/6 話 拼音 huà ㄏㄨㄚˋ

正體字	簡體字	手　寫	筆　順
話	话	話	話 話 話 話 話 話 話 話 話 話

甲骨文	金　文	小　篆
		𦧑

🔔 談論、述說：to talk about

　說話：to talk

🔔 言詞：expressions

　話語：words

　笑話：joke

> 他善於說笑話逗大家開心。
> He is good at telling jokes and making others happy.

8/7 高 拼音 gāo ㄍㄠ

正體字	簡體字	手寫
高	高	高

甲骨文	金文	小篆
𩫏	𩫏	高

筆順：高 高 高 高 高 高

📖 字像一座高的樓閣，用高樓來表示高：「高」resembles a high building. This character means tall or high.

高山：high mountains

🔔 價格貴的：high in price

高價：expensive

🔔 超越一般的水準：at a high level

高級：advanced, high level

> 她住的是高級住宅區。
> She lives in exclusive residential district.

8/8 低 拼音 dī ㄉㄧ

正體字	簡體字	手寫
低	低	低

甲骨文	金文	小篆
		低

筆順：低 低 低 低 低 低

🔔 上下距離小，或離地面近。與高相對：the opposite of "high"

降低：to lower, to reduce

🔔 俯、向下彎：to bend over

低頭：to lower one's head

🔔 低矮的：low, short

🔔 低聲：low voice

> 他低聲講話。
> He spoke in a low voice.

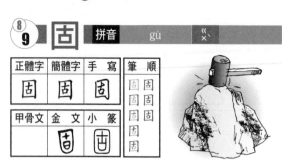

8/9 固　拼音　gù　ㄍㄨˋ

正體字	簡體字	手寫	筆　順
固	固	固	固 固
			固 固
甲骨文	**金　文**	**小　篆**	固 固
	固	固	固 固
			固

🔔 結實、堅硬：firm
　　穩固、堅固：steady

> 那把椅子相當穩固，可以站上去。
> That chair is firm enough to stand on.

🔔 堅決、堅持、極力：to be determined
　　固守：to hold on to

🔔 原來、一向：be inherent to
　　固有美德：traditional virtue

8/10 個　拼音　ge　ㄍㄜ

正體字	簡體字	手寫	筆　順
個	个	個	個 個
			個 個
甲骨文	**金　文**	**小　篆**	個 個
			個 個
			個 個

🔔 量詞，計算單獨的人或物的單位：a measure word for counting people or object
　　一個麵包： one piece of bread

🔔 單獨的：solitary (pronounced gè ㄍㄜˋ)
　　個性：personality

🔔 指特定對象的：determinative
　　這個：this
　　那個：that

> 這個人非常有個性。
> This man has a lot of personality.

⑧ 11 比 　拼音　bǐ　ㄅㄧˇ

正體字	簡體字	手寫	筆順
比	比	比	比 比 比 比

甲骨文	金文	小篆
𠤎	𠤎	𠤎

🔔 較量：to compare strength in a contest

　比賽：competition

> 我比你高
> I am taller than you.

🔔 依照、仿照：according to, to copy, to pattern after

　比照：contrast, according to

🔔 用手勢模擬動作：to gesticulate, to sign

　比手語：to perform sign language

⑧ 12 此 　拼音　cǐ　ㄘˇ

正體字	簡體字	手寫	筆順
此	此	此	此 此 此 此 此

甲骨文	金文	小篆
𣥂	𣥂	𣥂

🔔 這個：this

　此地：this place

> 此地不宜久留。
> This isn't a good place to stay for a long time.

　此人：this person

　此路不通：This road is blocked.

🔔 這樣：like this

　如此：in this way

⁸⁄₁₃ 些　拼音　xiē　ㄒㄧㄝ

正體字	簡體字	手寫	筆順
些	些	些	些 些 些 些 些 些 些

☆ 表示事物不確定的數量：small but uncertain quantity

> 有些：some
>
> 一些：a little

> 有些話不要說得太清楚，點到就好。
> It is not necessary to always be clear about what you say.

☆ 少量、一點：not much, a small amount

> 些微：a few, slightly

⁸⁄₁₄ 負　拼音　fù　ㄈㄨ

正體字	簡體字	手寫	筆順
負	负	負	負 負 負 負 負 負 負

☆ 承擔：to bear, to undertake

> 負責：be responsible for

> 他是一個負責、守信用的好先生。
> He is a good husband who is very responsible and always keeps his word.

☆ 自負：think highly of oneself

☆ 虧欠、拖欠：have a deficit, be in arrears

> 負債：be in debt

8 15 丙

| 拼音 | bǐng | ㄅㄧㄥˇ |

正體字	簡體字	手寫	筆順
丙	丙	丙	丙 丙 丙 丙 丙

甲骨文	金文	小篆
丙	丙	丙

用來排列次序等第，在甲、乙之後，表示第三：third, an ordinal number in Chinese after 甲 (first)、乙 (second)

丙班：the third class, Class 3

丙等：level 3

> 他的作業得了「丙」。
> He got a "C" on his homework.

火：fire

付丙：to burn

姓氏：a surname

8 16 病

| 拼音 | bìng | ㄅㄧㄥˋ |

正體字	簡體字	手寫	筆順
病	病	病	病病 病病 病病 病病 病病

甲骨文	金文	小篆
		病

指身體發生了不健康的現象：unhealthy, sick

生病：sick

肝病：hepatitis

> 生病了就要去看醫生。
> It is necessary to go to see a doctor when you get sick.

看病：to visit a doctor

病人：patient

8/17 痛 拼音 tòng ㄊㄨㄥˋ

正體字	簡體字	手寫	筆順
痛	痛	痛	痛痛痛 痛痛痛 痛痛 痛痛 痛痛

甲骨文	金 文	小 篆
		痛

🔔 疼痛：pain
　　頭痛：headache

🔔 悲傷：sad
　　悲痛：grieved

> 母親過世，讓我悲痛萬分。
> I am grieved by my mother's death.

🔔 盡情、徹底：fully enjoy, thoroughly
　　痛快：very happy

8/18 死 拼音 sǐ ㄙˇ

正體字	簡體字	手寫	筆順
死	死	死	死死 死 死 死 死

甲骨文	金 文	小 篆
𣦵	𣦵	𣦽

🔔 生命終止：the end of life
　　死亡：death

🔔 不通暢，靜止的：hindered
　　死胡同：dead alley
　　死水：dead water

🔔 毫無知覺，像死了一樣：totally unaware as if dead

> 他睡死了。
> He sleeps like the dead.

8/19 烏

| 拼音 | wū | × |

正體字	簡體字	手寫	筆順
烏	乌	烏	烏 烏 烏 烏 烏 烏 烏 烏 烏 烏

甲骨文	金 文	小 篆
	🜲	🜲

☼ 烏類：bird
　烏鴉：crow
☼ 黑色：black
　烏雲：dark cloud

> 烏雲密布，快要下雨了！
> The sky clouded over. It is going to rain.

☼ 烏合之眾：a disorderly crowd, a mob
☼ 烏克蘭：Ukraine
☼ 烏龍茶：oolong tea

8/20 鳥

| 拼音 | niǎo | ㄋㄧㄠˇ |

正體字	簡體字	手寫	筆順
鳥	鸟	鳥	鳥 鳥 鳥 鳥 鳥 鳥 鳥 鳥 鳥 鳥

甲骨文	金 文	小 篆
🐦	🐦	🐦

☼ 全身有羽毛、卵生，具有尖嘴的動物。：
　a creature that is covered with feathers and
　has a beak or a bill, and is oviparous.

　小鳥：birds
　鴕鳥：ostrich

> 清晨的山林，小鳥的歌聲特別響亮。
> The singing of birds is especially clear in
> the mountain forest in the early morning.

8/21 毛

拼音　máo　　ㄇㄠˊ

正體字	簡體字	手　寫	筆　順
毛	毛	毛	毛 毛 毛 毛
甲骨文	金　文	小　篆	
	￥	￥	

🔔 人和動物身上的毛髮：human hair or animal fur

羽毛：feather

眉毛：eyebrow

台灣藍鵲有修長又美麗的羽毛。
Formosan Blue Magpie has long, beautiful feathers.

🔔 姓氏：a surname

🔔 急躁的樣子：irritable

毛躁：short-tempered

8/22 們

拼音　men　　ㄇㄣ˙

正體字	簡體字	手　寫	筆　順
們	们	們	們 們 們 們 們 們 們 們 們 們
甲骨文	金　文	小　篆	

🔔 連接在名詞或人稱代名詞後面，表示複數：「們」is an adjunct to a noun or a personal pronoun to indicate plurality.

我們：we

他們：they

朋友們：friends

朋友們，我們準備出發囉！
Let's go, Friends.

正體字	簡體字	手 寫	筆 順
品	品	品	品 品

甲骨文	金 文	小 篆
吕	呂	吕

拼音　pǐn　ㄆㄧㄣˇ

🔔 某一類東西的總稱：a general name for a collection of things.

食品：food

🔔 人的德行：moral quality

人品：character

他的人品很好，不會在別人背後說閒話。
He has good personality. He doesn't speak ill of others behind their back.

🔔 評斷優劣：to test

品酒：wine tasting

正體字	簡體字	手 寫	筆 順
區	区	區	區 區

甲骨文	金 文	小 篆
品	品	區

拼音　qū　ㄑㄩ

🔔 表示一定的範圍：an area

住宅區：residential area

這裡是住宅區，環境幽雅。
This residential district is in an excellent area.

🔔 分別：to differentiate

區別：difference

區分：to differentiate

· 133 ·

8/25 先 拼音 xiān ㄒㄧㄢ

正體字	簡體字	手寫	筆順
先	先	先	先 先 先 先 先

甲骨文	金文	小篆
先	先	先

- 時間或次序在前：first, prior
  - 先前：before, previously
- 對已去世者的尊稱：a respectfully title for the dead
  - 先父：late father
- 對一般男子的尊稱：a respectfully title for men in general
  - 先生：mister

8/26 洗 拼音 xǐ ㄒㄧˇ

正體字	簡體字	手寫	筆順
洗	洗	洗	洗 洗 洗 洗 洗

甲骨文	金文	小篆
		洗

- 用水消除污垢：using water to remove dirt
  - 洗衣服：do the laundry
  - 我用洗衣機洗衣服。
I do the laundry in a washing machine.
  - 洗碗：to do the dishes
- 清除：to delete
  - 洗心革面：turn over a new leaf

(8/27) 快　拼音　kuài　ㄎㄨㄞˋ

正體字	簡體字	手　寫	筆　順
快	快	快	快 快 快 快 快 快

甲骨文	金　文	小　篆
		忄夬

🔔 開心、高興：It means happy and delighted.

　快樂：happiness

> 祝你生日快樂！
> Happy Birthday!

🔔 迅速：swift, rapid

　快速：fast
　快報：bulletin board
　快遞：express delivery

🔔 趕緊：to hurry up

　快點：to hurry up

(8/28) 慢　拼音　màn　ㄇㄢˋ

正體字	簡體字	手　寫	筆　順
慢	慢	慢	慢 慢 慢 慢 慢 慢 慢 慢 慢 慢 慢 慢 慢 慢

甲骨文	金　文	小　篆
		忄曼

🔔 怠惰：lazy

　怠慢：to neglect a visitor or guest

🔔 速度不快的：not fast

　慢跑：to jog
　慢工出細活：Take your time and do a good job.

> 我有慢跑的運動習慣。
> I jog for exercise.

🔔 驕傲、不禮貌：pride, proud, rude

　傲慢：arrogant

⑧29 冷 拼音 lěng ㄌㄥˇ

正體字	簡體字	手寫	筆順
冷	冷	冷	冷冷冷冷冷冷冷

甲骨文	金文	小篆
		冷

🔔 像冰一樣的寒冷：cold

  寒冷：cold, chilly

🔔 寂寞：lonely

  冷清：cold and cheerless, deserted

> 這場演唱會有些冷清。
> The concert was a little cold and cheerless.

🔔 諷刺的話語：irony, sarcasm

  冷言冷語：sarcastic comments

⑧30 熱 拼音 rè ㄖㄜˋ

正體字	簡體字	手寫	筆順
熱	热	熱	熱熱熱熱熱熱熱熱熱熱熱熱

甲骨文	金文	小篆
		熱

🔔 高溫度。與「冷」相對：high temperature

  「熱」is the opposite of cold.

  加熱：heating

🔔 受人喜愛的：popular, liked

  熱門：popular

🔔 強烈的：strong, intense

  熱愛：deep love, ardently love, love fervently

> 她熱愛文學勝過愛情。
> She loves literature more than love.

⑧31 巷

拼音 xiàng ㄒㄧㄤˋ

正體字	簡體字	手 寫
巷	巷	巷

甲骨文	金 文	小 篆
		蒼

筆 順
巷 巷
巷 巷
巷 巷
巷

⚜ 表示大街旁的小通道：lanes off main streets

大街小巷：streets and lanes

> 這項喜事，很快就傳遍大街小巷。
> The good news soon spread everywhere.

⚜ 街巷之間的：among the streets and lanes

街頭巷尾：everywhere

巷戰：street fight

*9*月
September

⑨1 港 拼音 gǎng ㄍㄤˇ

正體字	簡體字	手寫
港	港	港

筆 順
港 港 港 港 港 港 港 港 港 港 港 港 港 港 港

甲骨文	金 文	小 篆
		灡

🔔 河流或海灣深曲處，可以停泊船隻的口岸：part of a body of water deep enough to provide anchorage for ships

海港：harbor

港口：harbor

🔔 **香港**：Hong Kong

> 我們學校有不少來自香港的學生。
> Many students in our school come from Hong Kong.

⑨2 和 拼音 hé ㄏㄜˊ

正體字	簡體字	手寫
和	和	和

筆 順
和 和 和 和 和 和 和 和

甲骨文	金 文	小 篆
	𬇙	𪛇

🔔 各數相加的總數：a sum total

總和：the sum

🔔 溫暖的：warm

和煦：pleasantly warm

> 風暖花開，天氣和煦。
> Flowers are blooming. The weather is pleasantly warm.

🔔 一起：to be together

我和你：you and me

🔔 **和睦相處**：live together in peace

⑨3 加　拼音　jiā　ㄐㄧㄚ

正體字	簡體字	手　寫	筆　順
加	加	加	加 加 加 加 加

甲骨文	金　文	小　篆	
	𠃌	𠨍	

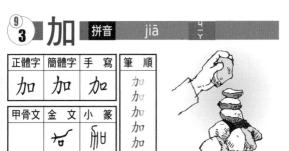

🔔 增加：to increase

　增加：to increase

　加班：to work overtime

🔔 兩個數目的結合：to add, addition

> 三加五等於八
> Three plus five is eight.

⑨4 四　拼音　sì　ㄙˋ

正體字	簡體字	手　寫	筆　順
四	四	四	四 四 四 四 四

甲骨文	金　文	小　篆	
	𝕏	𝕏	

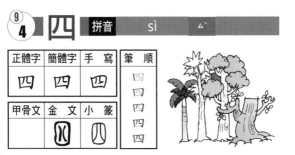

🔔 數量詞「四」：the number four

　四棵樹：four trees

> 植樹節，我種了四棵樹。
> I planted four trees on Arbor Day.

🔔 次序排第四的：「四」could also be used
as an ordinal number, fourth.

　第四：fourth

> 四月是一年中的第四個月。
> April is the fourth month of the year.

⑨5 肆 　拼音　sì　ㄙˋ

正體字	簡體字	手　寫
肆	肆	肆

筆　順
肆 肆 肆
肆 肆 肆
肆 肆 肆
肆 肆
肆 肆

甲骨文	金　文	小　篆
		肆

- 四的大寫：long formal version of four used by banks to prevent fraud
  - 肆萬元：forty thousand dollars
- 放縱，沒有拘束：indulge, not restrict
  - 放肆：unbridled, wanton
- 任意、放縱：wantonly, indulge
  - 肆無忌憚：act recklessly and care for nobody, afraid of nothing, outrageously

⑨6 半 　拼音　bàn　ㄅㄢˋ

正體字	簡體字	手　寫
半	半	半

筆　順
半
半
半
半

甲骨文	金　文	小　篆
	半	半

- 二分之一：half
  - 半數：half the number
  - 半個：half of something

> 投票結果，超過半數同意此意見。
> Through voting, it was shown that more than half the people agreed to this suggestion.

- 在……中間：in the middle of something
  - 半夜：in the middle of the night

⁹₇ 伴　拼音　bàn　ㄅㄢˋ

正體字	簡體字	手寫	筆　順
伴	伴	伴	伴伴 伴伴 伴伴 伴

甲骨文	金文	小篆
		伴

📖 左邊一個「人」，右邊一個「半」，表示有人陪同：「伴」consists of the left part,「人」(person) and the right part「半」. It means to have somebody for company.

🔅 陪伴：to accompany

🔅 在一起而能互相幫助的人：a person who is always available to offer help

　伴侶：partner, companion

> 他需要一個伴侶和他共享生活。
> He needs a partner to share his life.

⁹₈ 家　拼音　jiā　ㄐㄧㄚ

正體字	簡體字	手寫	筆　順
家	家	家	家家 家家 家家 家家

甲骨文	金文	小篆
宀	宀	家

🔅 人居住的地方：a residence

　家庭：family

> 我擁有一個溫馨的家庭。
> I have a loving family.

🔅 有專門技術的人：a person with expertise

　科學家：scientist

🔅 量詞：a measure word

　三家商店：three shops

⑨9 休 拼音 xiū ㄒㄧㄡ

正體字	簡體字	手寫	筆順
休	休	休	休 休 休 休 休

甲骨文	金文	小篆
休	休	休

🔔 歇息：rest

　　休養、休憩：to take a rest

> 休息是為了走更長遠的路。
> He took a rest so he'd be able to go farther on.

🔔 終止：to suspend, to cease

　　休學：to suspend one's schooling

🔔 辭退官職、工作：to withdraw from one's position

　　退休：to retire

⑨10 成 拼音 chéng ㄔㄥˊ

正體字	簡體字	手寫	筆順
成	成	成	成 成 成 成 成

甲骨文	金文	小篆
成	成	成

🔔 做好事情：「成」indicates accomplishing something.

　　完成：to accomplish, finish

> 他希望有大成就。
> He hopes to achieve something great.

🔔 完整的：complete

　　成天：a whole day

🔔 促成：facilitate

　　成全：to help someone achieve his aim

9/11 城 拼音 chéng ㄔㄥˊ

正體字	簡體字	手 寫	筆 順
城	城	城	城城 城城 城城 城

甲骨文	金 文	小 篆
	戓	城

🔔 古時環繞京師或圍繞某一區域以供防守的
大圍牆：city walls

城牆：city wall

🔔 都市：city, urban

城市：city

> 台北市是一個世界級的城市。
> Taipei is a world-class city.

9/12 市 拼音 shì ㄕˋ

正體字	簡體字	手 寫	筆 順
市	市	市	市 市 市 市

甲骨文	金 文	小 篆
	芾	市

🔔 進行買賣、交易的地方：「市」is a place
for people to buy and sell things.

市場：market

超市：supermarket

🔔 人口密集、工商業發達的城鎮：a town/
city with a dense population

都市：city

🔔 行政區劃分的單位：an administrative unit

台北市：Taipei city

9 / 13　寺

拼音　　sì　　ㄙ

正體字	簡體字	手寫
寺	寺	寺

甲骨文	金文	小篆
	ㄓ	寺

筆順：寺 寺 寺 寺 寺 寺

📢 佛教的廟宇，僧人所居住的地方：Buddhist temples

寺廟：temple

這座寺廟建築得古色古香。
The temple is in an ancient style.

9 / 14　侍

拼音　　shì　　ㄕ

正體字	簡體字	手寫
侍	侍	侍

甲骨文	金文	小篆
		侍

筆順：侍 侍 侍 侍 侍 侍 侍 侍

📢 伺候：to wait upon, to serve

服侍：to wait upon, to serve, to attend

📢 服侍或隨從他人的人：a person who attends to or takes care of somebody

侍從、侍衛：attendants

侍者：waiter

女侍者：waitress

我請假在家裡服侍生病的母親。
I asked for leave to attend to my sick mother.

⑨15 待 拼音 dài ㄉㄞˋ

正體字	簡體字	手寫	筆順
待	待	待	待 待 待 待 待 待 待 待 待

甲骨文	金文	小篆
	𢓊	待

🔔 等候：to wait

　等待：to wait

🔔 對待、照顧：to treat, to take care of

　招待：to entertain, receive (somebody)

　優待：preferential treatment

感謝你熱忱的招待！
Thank you for your enthusiastic reception.

⑨16 池 拼音 chí ㄔˊ

正體字	簡體字	手寫	筆順
池	池	池	池 池 池 池 池 池 池

甲骨文	金文	小篆

🔔 水池：pond

　游泳池：swimming pool

夏天最適合泡在游泳池裡解熱。
Summer is the perfect time to soak in a swimming pool to keep cool.

🔔 姓氏：a surname

9 / 17 她 拼音 tā ㄊㄚ

正體字	簡體字	手 寫	筆 順
她	她	她	她 她 她 她 她

甲骨文	金 文	小 篆

🔔 女性的第三人稱代名詞：third personal feminine pronoun

> 她是我的母親。
> She is my mother.

9 / 18 他 拼音 tā ㄊㄚ

正體字	簡體字	手 寫	筆 順
他	他	他	他 他 他 他

甲骨文	金 文	小 篆

🔔 第三人稱：third personal male pronoun
🔔 他人：others

> 他是一位老師。
> He is a teacher.

🔔 另外的：other, another
他日：another day

9/19 牠 拼音 tā ㄊㄚ

正體字	簡體字	手 寫	筆 順
牠	它	牠	牠牠牠牠牠牠
甲骨文	金 文	小 篆	

🔔 動物的第三人稱代名詞：third personal pronoun for animals

> 牠是我們家養的小狗。
> It is our dog.

9/20 祂 拼音 tā ㄊㄚ

正體字	簡體字	手 寫	筆 順
祂	祂	祂	祂祂祂祂祂祂
甲骨文	金 文	小 篆	

🔔 對上天、神明的第三人稱代名詞：third personal pronoun for the deities

> 信祂得永生。
> Believe in God and have the eternal life.

9/21 是　拼音　shì　ㄕˋ

正體字	簡體字	手寫
是	是	是

甲骨文	金文	小篆
	旱	昰

```
458
 37
+121
616
```

🔔 正確：correct

　　自以為是：be opinionated

🔔 肯定的話語：a positive utterance

　　滿身是汗：sweaty all over

🔔 存在的事實：an existing fact

　她是老師。
　She is a teacher.

9/22 斥　拼音　chì　ㄔˋ

正體字	簡體字	手寫
斥	斥	斥

甲骨文	金文	小篆

🔔 排除拒絕、摒棄不用：to exclude

　　排斥：to repel

　不要排斥和自己意見不同的人。
　Do not push away those who have
　different opinions from yours.

🔔 責罵：to scold

　　痛斥：to denounce

🔔 動用，出：to put something to use

　　斥資：to spend, to allocate funds

9/23 拆 拼音 chāi ㄔㄞ

正體字	簡體字	手 寫	筆 順
拆	拆	拆	拆 拆 拆 拆 拆 拆 拆

甲骨文	金 文	小 篆

分開、打開：to separate, to open

拆開：to unpack

拆散：to separate

我拆開信封閱讀信件。
I opened the letter and started reading.

9/24 折 拼音 zhé ㄓㄜˊ

正體字	簡體字	手 寫	筆 順
折	折	折	折 折 折 折 折 折 折

甲骨文	金 文	小 篆
𣂗	𣂗	𣂗

摘取、弄斷：to pick, to break

折斷：to break

彎曲：to bend

曲折：to twist, to complicate

折扣：to discount

五折：50% off

百貨公司現在有五折優待的商品。
Some products at the department stores are now fifty percent off.

七折：30% off

9/25 存 拼音 cún ㄘㄨㄣˊ

正體字	簡體字	手寫
存	存	存

甲骨文	金文	小篆
		㘰

筆順：存 存 存 存

🔔 存在、生存：to exist, to survive

魚需要水才能生存。
Fish need water to live.

🔔 寄放：to leave something with...
寄存：to deposit

🔔 儲蓄：to deposit
存款：savings

9/26 李 拼音 lǐ ㄌㄧˇ

正體字	簡體字	手寫
李	李	李

甲骨文	金文	小篆
	𣏟	𣏟

筆順：李 李 李 李 李

🔔 一種植物的果實，可當作水果食用：the fruit of a plant
李子：plum

我喜歡吃李子。
I like to eat plums.

🔔 姓氏：a surname

9/27 季 拼音 jì ㄐㄧˋ

正體字	簡體字	手 寫	筆 順
季	季	季	季季季 季季 季季 季

甲骨文	金 文	小 篆

🔔 計時的名稱。一季有三個月。：a unit of time. There are three months in one season.

春季：spring

季節：season

這個季節天氣都不錯。
The weather is nice this time of the year.

🔔 一個固定的時期：a certain period of time

花季：florescent season

雨季： rainy season

9/28 肉 拼音 ròu ㄖㄡˋ

正體字	簡體字	手 寫	筆 順
肉	肉	肉	肉肉 肉 肉 肉

甲骨文	金 文	小 篆

🔔 動物體中包住骨骼的柔韌物質：meat, flesh

肌肉：muscle

牛肉：beef

🔔 蔬果除去皮核的部分：the part of fruit after removing skin

果肉：pulp

🔔 身體。與「精神」相對：flesh, the opposite of "spirit"

肉身：corporeal body

9/29 臉　拼音　liǎn　ㄌㄧㄢˇ

正體字	簡體字	手　寫
臉	脸	臉

筆　順
臉臉臉臉
臉臉臉臉
臉臉臉
臉臉臉
臉臉臉

甲骨文	金　文	小　篆

🔔 面部：face
　　洗臉：to wash the face
🔔 面子：face
　　丟臉：to lose face
🔔 面部的表情：facial expression
　　翻臉：to have fallen out

他是一個翻臉不認人的人。
He is a person who turns against friends.

9/30 儉　拼音　jiǎn　ㄐㄧㄢˇ

正體字	簡體字	手　寫
儉	俭	儉

筆　順
儉儉儉
儉儉儉
儉儉儉
儉儉儉
儉儉儉

甲骨文	金　文	小　篆
		儉

🔔 節約：frugal, thrifty, economize, economical
　　節儉：frugal
　　勤儉：hardworking and thrifty

我們過著節儉的生活。
We lead a frugal life.

*10*月
October

檢 拼音 jiǎn ㄐㄧㄢˇ

正體字	簡體字	手寫
檢	检	檢

甲骨文	金文	小篆
		檢

筆順
檢檢檢檢
檢檢檢檢
檢檢檢
檢檢檢
檢檢檢

🔔 查驗：to check, to examine

   檢查：to inspect, to examine

🔔 約束：to restrain, to keep within bounds

   行為不檢：indiscreet

🔔 揭發：to expose

   檢舉：to report an offense to the authorities

檢舉不法行為，才能打擊犯罪。
Reporting offences to the authorities is the only way to crack down on crime.

面 拼音 miàn ㄇㄧㄢˋ

正體字	簡體字	手寫
面	面	面

甲骨文	金文	小篆
		面

筆順
面面
面面
面面
面面
面

🔔 人的臉：the human face

   面貌：face, features, looks

   失面子：to lose face

🔔 物體的外表或上部的一層：the appearance or the top of an object

   水面：the surface of the water

🔔 量詞，計算平面物的單位：a measuring term; a unit used for calculating things with flat surface

   一面旗子：a flag

10/3 答 拼音 dá ㄉㄚˊ

正體字	簡體字	手 寫	筆 順
答	答	答	答答答 答答答 答答答 答答
甲骨文	金 文	小 篆	

🔔 回覆別人的問題：to reply to questions

　回答：to answer

> 我很有禮貌的回答他的問題。
> I answered his questions politely.

🔔 接受他人的恩惠而加以回報：to accept a favor from the others and repay for it

　報答：to repay

🔔 答應：to respond, to promise (pronounced dā ㄉㄚ)

10/4 保 拼音 bǎo ㄅㄠˇ

正體字	簡體字	手 寫	筆 順
保	保	保	保保 保保 保保 保保 保
甲骨文	金 文	小 篆	
保	保	保	

🔔 養護：to maintain

　保養：to take good care of

> 她很懂得保養自己的身體。
> She knows how to take good care of her health.

🔔 承擔：to bear, to undertake

　保險：insurance

🔔 伙計、員工：staff, personnel

　酒保：bartender

⑩5 堡 拼音 bǎo ㄅㄠˇ

正體字	簡體字	手寫
堡	堡	堡

甲骨文	金文	小篆

筆順
堡 堡 堡
堡 堡 堡
堡 堡 堡
堡 堡

- 用土石築成的小城：a small town built with dirt and rocks

  城堡：castle

- 工事堅固的陣地：a building built in order to defend an area against attack

  碉堡：blockhouse, fort

  這是戰爭留下來的碉堡。
  This is an old blockhouse left behind from the war.

⑩6 相 拼音 xiàng ㄒㄧㄤˋ

正體字	簡體字	手寫
相	相	相

甲骨文	金文	小篆
𣐽	𣐽	相

筆順
相 相
相 相
相 相
相

- 容貌、外形、模樣：appearance, looks

  長相：looks

- 彼此、交互，兩方面都進行的：each other, two aspects both carry on (pronounced xiāng ㄒㄧㄤ)

  相親相愛：love each other

  他們兄弟倆很相親相愛。
  The two brothers love each other devotedly.

10/7 想　拼音　xiǎng　ㄒㄧㄤˇ

正體字	簡體字	手 寫	筆 順
想	想	想	想 想 想 想 想 想 想 想 想 想 想 想 想

甲骨文	金 文	小 篆
		想

☆ 思考：to think

想辦法：to think over a problem, to think of a way

> 我會想辦法解決這個問題。
> I will find a solution to solve the problem.

☆ 要、希望：to want, to hope, to wish

理想：ideal

☆ 思念、懷念：to think of, to miss

想念：miss

10/8 兩　拼音　liǎng　ㄌㄧㄤˇ

正體字	簡體字	手 寫	筆 順
兩	两	兩	兩 兩 兩 兩 兩 兩 兩

甲骨文	金 文	小 篆
	兩	兩

☆ 計算重量的單位：a unit of weight

一兩：a tael

☆ 當作數目字「二」，表示一對、一雙的意思：It can be used as the number of two. It represents a pair of things.

兩隻老虎：two tigers

☆ 雙方、彼此：the two parties, each other

兩敗俱傷：Both sides suffered great losses.

兩相情願：Both sides are willing.

⑩9 輛 拼音 liàng ㄌㄧㄤˋ

正體字	簡體字	手寫
輛	辆	輛

甲骨文	金文	小篆

筆順
輛輛輛
輛輛輛
輛輛輛
輛輛輛
輛輛輛

量詞，是計算車子的單位：a unit of measure, a measure word for vehicles

一輛車子：a car

我們共同搭乘一輛車子去上班。
We take the same car to work.

⑩10 汁 拼音 zhī ㄓ

正體字	簡體字	手寫
汁	汁	汁

甲骨文	金文	小篆
		汁

筆順
汁
汁
汁
汁
汁

物體中所含的水分、液體：liquid from certain objects

果汁：juice
肉汁：gravy

我喝自己做的果汁當作早餐。
I drink juice I make for breakfast.

⑩ 11 針 拼音 zhēn ㄓㄣ

正體字	簡體字	手 寫	筆 順
針	针	針	針針針針 針針針針 針針針針 針針針針 針針針針

甲骨文	金 文	小 篆

用來引線縫紉、刺繡或編結的工具：the needles used to sew, embroider, or knit

毛線針：knitting needle

尖銳似針形的東西：needle-like objects

大頭針：pin

打針：to give injection

> 中國的針灸很神奇。
> Chinese acupuncture is mysterious.

⑩ 12 登 拼音 dēng ㄉㄥ

正體字	簡體字	手 寫	筆 順
登	登	登	登登登 登登登 登登登 登登登 登登

甲骨文	金 文	小 篆

由低處到高處：to climb

登山：mountain climbing

記錄、刊載：to record, publish

登記：to register

刊登：to post

> 這篇文章刊登在報紙上。
> This article was posted in a renowned newspaper.

10 / 13 燈

拼音 dēng ㄉㄥ

正體字	簡體字	手 寫
燈	灯	燈

甲骨文	金 文	小 篆

筆 順
燈燈燈燈
燈燈燈
燈燈燈
燈燈燈
燈燈燈

照明或作為發光的器具：a thing that gives or produces light

電燈：light

紅綠燈：traffic light

愛迪生發明電燈。
Thomas Alva Edison invented the electric light.

用來加熱的器具：a tool used to heat things

酒精燈：alcohol burner

10 / 14 妹

拼音 mèi ㄇㄟˋ

正體字	簡體字	手 寫
妹	妹	妹

甲骨文	金 文	小 篆
𣱛	㛒	𣑥

筆 順
妹妹
妹妹
妹妹
妹
妹

稱呼年齡比自己小的女生：younger female sibling

妹妹：younger sister

我的妹妹很受家人的寵愛。
All family members dote on my younger sister.

⑩15 姐 | 拼音 jiě | ㄐㄧㄝˇ

正體字	簡體字	手寫	筆順
姐	姐	姐	姐 姐 姐 姐 姐 姐 姐 姐

甲骨文	金文	小篆
		姐

🔔 稱呼親戚中長於自己的同輩女性：elder sister

姐姐：elder sister

🔔 指年輕的女子：young lady

小姐：Miss

> 請問小姐貴姓芳名？
> May I ask your name, Miss?

⑩16 受 | 拼音 shòu | ㄕㄡˋ

正體字	簡體字	手寫	筆順
受	受	受	受 受 受 受 受 受 受 受

甲骨文	金文	小篆

🔔 收到、接獲：to receive, to get

接受：to accept

🔔 容納、容忍：to contain, to hold, tolerance

承受：to bear

> 丈夫突然車禍過世，她無法承受這樣的傷痛。
> Her husband suddenly passed away in a car accident. She cannot bear the pain.

🔔 被、遭到：passive voice, to suffer

受驚：frightened

10 / 17　愛　拼音　ài　ㄞˋ

正體字	簡體字	手寫
愛	爱	愛

甲骨文	金文	小篆
		𤔰

筆順：愛

- 🔔 喜歡：like
  - 愛情：love
- 🔔 兩個人彼此喜歡的感情：fond of each other
  - 愛女：beloved daughter
- 🔔 被寵愛的人事物：beloved
  - 愛車：beloved car

> 這是我新購買的愛車。
> This is my beloved car that I just purchased not long ago.

10 / 18　情　拼音　qíng　ㄑㄧㄥˊ

正體字	簡體字	手寫
情	情	情

甲骨文	金文	小篆
		情

筆順：情

- 🔔 感情：emotion
  - 心情：mood

> 不要太感情用事。
> Don't be too emotional.

- 🔔 實際的狀況：real situation
  - 事情：affair

⑩ 19 精 拼音 jīng ㄐㄧㄥ

正體字	簡體字	手 寫
精	精	精

筆 順
精精精
精精精
精精精
精精精
精精

甲骨文	金 文	小 篆
		精

🔔 提煉的：refined
  精鹽：refined salt

🔔 擅長：be good at
  精通：be good at

他精通五種語言。
He has mastered five languages.

🔔 細緻的：fine
  精密：precision

⑩ 20 重 拼音 zhòng ㄓㄨㄥˋ

正體字	簡體字	手 寫
重	重	重

筆 順
重重
重重
重重
重

甲骨文	金 文	小 篆
	重	重

🔔 物體或人體的分量：weight
  體重：weight

保持適當的體重，是健康的第一要素。
The most important thing to stay healthy is to maintain an appropriate body weight.

🔔 尊敬：respect
  尊重：respect

🔔 再一次：again (pronounced chóng ㄔㄨㄥˊ)
  重複：to repeat

ⁱ⁰/21 輕 拼音 qīng ㄑㄧㄥ

正體字	簡體字	手寫	筆順
輕	轻	輕	輕輕輕 輕輕輕 輕輕輕 輕輕輕 輕輕

甲骨文	金文	小篆
		輕

🔔 物體的重量小：of little weight

　輕巧：light and handy

🔔 方便的：convenient

　輕便：light and portable

> 我穿著休閒服去郊遊。
> I dressed casually for the outing.

🔔 隨便、不莊重：not dignified

　輕率：imprudent

ⁱ⁰/22 前 拼音 qián ㄑㄧㄢˊ

正體字	簡體字	手寫	筆順
前	前	歬	前前 前前 前前 前前 前

甲骨文	金文	小篆
	肯	肯

🔔 行進：to march forward

　前進：to go forward

🔔 過去的：in the past

　前天：the day before yesterday

> 前天是我們的結婚紀念日。
> Our wedding anniversary was the day before yesterday.

🔔 未來的：in the future

　前途：future

10/23 後 拼音 hòu ㄏㄡˋ

正體字	簡體字	手 寫	筆 順
後	后	後	後 後 後 後 後 後 後 後 後 後

甲骨文	金 文	小 篆

🔔 時間上較晚的：at a later time

  後來：later

🔔 在空間、位置上，與「前」相對：the opposite of "front"

  後面：back

> 後面的椅子是空的。
> The chair in the back is empty.

🔔 次序、位置接近末尾的：near the end in terms of sequence or position

  後門：back door

10/24 細 拼音 xì ㄒㄧˋ

正體字	簡體字	手 寫	筆 順
細	细	細	細 細 細 細 細 細 細 細 細 細 細

甲骨文	金 文	小 篆
		細

🔔 微小：small, tiny

  細沙：fine sand

🔔 周密：careful, thorough

  細心：careful

> 他做事情很細心。
> He does things very carefully.

🔔 瑣碎的：trifling, trivial, miscellaneous

  細節：details

10/25 粗

| 拼音 | cū | ㄘ ㄨ |

正體字	簡體字	手 寫
粗	粗	粗

甲骨文	金 文	小 篆
		粗

筆 順

粗 粗 粗
粗 粗
粗 粗
粗 粗
粗 粗

🔔 疏忽、不周密：carelessness

粗心：careless

🔔 不精緻：not delicate

粗糙：coarse

🔔 不文雅：not cultured

粗魯：rude

這種粗魯的行為不可取。
Coarse behavior like this is not desirable.

10/26 雨

| 拼音 | yǔ | ㄩˇ |

正體字	簡體字	手 寫
雨	雨	雨

甲骨文	金 文	小 篆
		雨

筆 順

雨 雨
雨 雨
雨 雨
雨
雨

🔔 天上落下來的水：rain

下雨：rain

最近下午容易下雨。
It has been raining a lot in the afternoon lately.

她在雨中漫步。
She is walking in the rain.

10/27 雪

拼音	xuě	ㄒㄩㄝˇ

正體字	簡體字	手 寫		筆 順
雪	雪	雪		雪雪雪 雪雪雪 雪雪雪 雪雪雪 雪雪雪
甲骨文	金 文	小 篆		
𩂣				

🔔 下雪：to snow

> 屋外正在大雪紛飛。
> It is snowing heavily outside.

🔔 如雪一般白色的：as white as snow

> 雪白：snow white

🔔 洗刷、洗清、清除：to wash off, clean oneself of, clean up

> 雪恥：wipe out a humiliation or disgrace

10/28 杯

拼音	bēi	ㄅㄟ

正體字	簡體字	手 寫		筆 順
杯	杯	杯		杯杯 杯杯 杯杯 杯 杯
甲骨文	金 文	小 篆		

🔔 裝液體的容器：container for holding liquid

> 杯子：cup

> 這個陶瓷杯子，很具特色。
> This ceramic cup is unique.

🔔 量詞，是計算杯裝物的單位：a measure word for things in cups or glasses

> 一杯水：a glass of water

10/29 湯 拼音 tāng ㄊㄤ

正體字	簡體字	手寫
湯	汤	湯

甲骨文	金文	小篆
	煬	湯

筆順
湯湯湯
湯湯湯
湯湯
湯湯
湯湯

🔔 食物加水烹煮之後的汁液：soup

　　雞湯：chicken soup

🔔 姓氏：a surname

> 湯先生很喜歡喝香菇雞湯。
> Mr. Tang likes chicken soup with mushrooms.

10/30 舌 拼音 shé ㄕㄜˊ

正體字	簡體字	手寫
舌	舌	舌

甲骨文	金文	小篆

筆順
舌舌
舌
舌
舌
舌

🔔 味覺器官：tongue

　　舌頭：tongue

> 他的舌頭被熱湯燙到。
> He burned his tongue drinking hot soup.

🔔 物體像舌頭的部分：shaped like a tongue

　　火舌：flame

　　帽舌：visor

甘　拼音　gān　ㄍㄢ

正體字	簡體字	手 寫
甘	甘	甘

甲骨文	金 文	小 篆
甘	甘	甘

筆 順
甘
甘
甘
甘

🔔 甜美的：sweet

甘甜：taste sweet

> 這水果真是美味甘甜。
> This fruit is tasty and sweet.

🔔 意、情願、自願：be willing to

甘願：be willing to

甘拜下風：bow to somebody's superiority

🔔 姓氏：a surname

11月
November

甜

拼音	tián	ㄊㄧㄢˊ

正體字	簡體字	手　寫	筆　順
甜	甜	甜	甜 甜 甜 甜 甜 甜 甜 甜 甜 甜

甲骨文	金　文	小　篆
		甛

⏾ 像糖的味道：sweet

> 水果真甜。
> This fruit is really sweet.

⏾ 美好：wonderful

> 甜蜜：sugary, honey

> 甜美：sweet

> 這種果實碩大而甜美。
> The fruit is very large and sweet.

⏾ 安穩：smooth and steady

> 睡得很甜：to sleep like a baby

苦

拼音	kǔ	ㄎㄨˇ

正體字	簡體字	手　寫	筆　順
苦	苦	苦	苦 苦 苦 苦 苦 苦 苦 苦 苦

甲骨文	金　文	小　篆
		苦

⏾ 味道的一種，和「甜」相反：「苦」is the opposite of sweet.

> 苦瓜：bitter melon

> 藥真是又苦又難吃的東西。
> Medicine is bitter and tastes awful.

⏾ 難以忍受的情況：unbearable situation

> 苦日子：hard times

⏾ 盡心盡力的：to make an all-out effort

> 埋頭苦幹：to bury oneself in work

11/3 若 拼音 ruò ㄖㄨ

正體字	簡體字	手寫	筆順
若	若	若	若 若 若 若 若 若 若 若 若

甲骨文	金文	小篆
𦫳	𦫳	𦫳

🔔 如果、假如：if, in case

假若：if, in case

門庭若市：be crowded with visitors

這家店門庭若市。
The store was crowded.

🔔 好像：seem, be like

欣喜若狂：go wild with joy

11/4 切 拼音 qiè ㄑㄧㄝ

正體字	簡體字	手寫	筆順
切	切	切	切 切 切 切

甲骨文	金文	小篆
		㘡

🔔 密合：close

親切：kind

🔔 所有的：all

一切：all, everything

🔔 把事物切斷：to cut (pronounced qiē ㄑㄧㄝ)

切菜：to cut up vegetables

切菜時要注意菜刀的使用。
Be careful how you use the knife when cutting vegetables.

⑪5 厚 拼音 hòu ㄏㄡˋ

正體字	簡體字	手 寫	筆 順
厚	厚	厚	厚 厚 厚 厚 厚 厚 厚 厚 厚

甲骨文	金 文	小 篆
厚	厚	厚

🔔 扁平物體上下之間距離較大的：thick

厚衣服：thick clothes

厚紙：thick paper

> 冬天穿著厚衣裳。
> In winter, we wear heavy colthes.

🔔 不刻薄的：not mean

忠厚：honest and tolerant

🔔 優待：privilege

厚待：to favor

⑪6 薄 拼音 bó ㄅㄛˊ

正體字	簡體字	手 寫	筆 順
薄	薄	薄	薄 薄 薄 薄 薄 薄 薄 薄 薄 薄 薄 薄 薄 薄 薄 薄 薄 薄 薄

甲骨文	金 文	小 篆
		薄

🔔 厚度小：not thick

薄片：thin slice

> 這是一張薄紙。
> This is a thin sheet of paper.

🔔 不尊重：disrespect

輕薄：frivolous

🔔 不寬厚：not generous

刻薄：unkind, harsh, mean

> 刻薄對待別人，對自己並沒有好處。
> You don't get anything out of being harsh.

11/7 歌　拼音　gē　《さ

正體字	簡體字	手　寫
歌	歌	歌

筆　順
歌歌歌 歌歌歌 歌歌歌 歌歌歌 歌歌

甲骨文	金　文	小　篆
		謌

🔔 唱：to sing
　　唱歌：to sing a song
🔔 搭配音樂的，供人歌唱的作品：song
　　歌曲：song

> 這首愛情歌曲扣人心弦。
> This love song is touching.

11/8 曲　拼音　qū　く凵

正體字	簡體字	手　寫
曲	曲	曲

筆　順
曲曲 曲 曲 曲

甲骨文	金　文	小　篆
𠃊	𠚊	曲

🔔 彎曲：bend
　　曲線：curve
🔔 勉強的：reluctant
　　委曲：crooked
🔔 歌曲：song (pronounced qǔ 〈凵)
　　作曲：to compose
　　作曲家：composer

> 貝多芬是一位古典音樂作曲家。
> Beethoven was a classical composer.

11/9 睡

拼音	shuì	ㄕㄨㄟˋ

正體字	簡體字	手 寫
睡	睡	睡

甲骨文	金 文	小 篆
		睡

筆 順
睡睡睡
睡睡睡
睡睡睡
睡睡睡
睡睡

☆ 閉上眼睛，身體呈現一個休息的狀態：
sleep

睡覺：to sleep

睡眠：to fall asleep

> 睡眠不足有礙健康。
> Not having enough sleep is bad for health.

☆ 睡眠時用的：used while one is sleeping

睡衣：pajamas

11/10 醒

拼音	xǐng	ㄒㄧㄥˇ

正體字	簡體字	手 寫
醒	醒	醒

甲骨文	金 文	小 篆
		醒

筆 順
醒醒醒醒
醒醒醒
醒醒醒
醒醒醒
醒醒醒

☆ 結束睡眠的狀態：to end sleep

睡醒：to wake up

☆ 酒醉或昏迷後恢復正常：to return to a normal state of consciousness after being drunk or in a coma

清醒：clear-minded, awake

> 早晨是頭腦最清醒的時候。
> The brain is clearest in the morning.

☆ 覺悟、明白：awareness, to understand

醒悟：to realize the truth

11/11 魚 拼音 yú ㄩˊ

正體字	簡體字	手 寫
魚	鱼	魚

甲骨文	金 文	小 篆

筆 順
魚 魚 魚
魚 魚
魚 魚
魚 魚
魚 魚

水生脊椎動物的總稱：general name of aquatic vertebrates
- 金魚：goldfish
- 鯨魚：whale
- 鱷魚：crocodile

體型像魚的東西：objects shaped like a fish
- 木魚：wooden fish

11/12 游 拼音 yóu ㄧㄡˊ

正體字	簡體字	手 寫
游	游	游

甲骨文	金 文	小 篆

筆 順
游 游 游
游 游 游
游 游
游 游
游 游

人或動物在水中行動：to swim
- 游泳：to swim

我用游泳來減重。
I swim to lose weight.

河流的段落：section of a river
- 上游：upper reaches
- 中游：middle reaches
- 下游：lower reaches

11/13 遊

拼音　yóu　一ㄡˊ

正體字	簡體字	手　寫
遊	遊	遊

甲骨文	金　文	小　篆
	𣎴	

筆　順

遊 遊 遊
遊 遊 遊
遊 遊 遊
遊 遊
遊 遊

🔔 遊蕩：to wander

🔔 旅遊：to travel

> 我利用假期到處去旅遊。
> I go traveling on holidays.

🔔 自由運轉：to operate freely

遊刃有餘：to do something skillfully and easily

11/14 園

拼音　yuán　ㄩㄢˊ

正體字	簡體字	手　寫
園	园	園

甲骨文	金　文	小　篆
		𠨑

筆　順

園 園 園
園 園 園
園 園 園
園 園 園
園 園

🔔 種植花木、蔬果的地方：a plot of ground where flowers and vegetables are cultivated

菜園：kitchen garden

🔔 讓人遊玩、休息的地方：a place where one can relax and have fun

公園：park

遊樂園：amusement park

> 我有自己的菜園。
> I have my own kitchen garden.

¹¹/15 遠 | 拼音 | yuǎn | ㄩㄢˇ

正體字	簡體字	手　寫
遠	远	遠

甲骨文	金　文	小　篆
	𤕦	遠

筆　順
遠 遠 遠 遠 遠 遠 遠 遠 遠 遠 遠 遠 遠 遠

🔔 形容時間、空間的距離很大：distant in time or space

遙遠：far

在遙遠的地方，有我思念的人。
Somewhere far away, there is a person I am missing.

🔔 形容很難懂的知識：hard to describe or understand

深遠：profound

¹¹/16 近 | 拼音 | jìn | ㄐㄧㄣˋ

正體字	簡體字	手　寫
近	近	近

甲骨文	金　文	小　篆
		近

筆　順
近 近 近 近 近 近 近 近 近 近

🔔 距離小：close to

附近：in the vicinity, nearby

我家附近是社區的公園。
There is a park in my neighborhood.

🔔 親密：intimate

親近：be close to

🔔 時間、地點、血統、關係等方面距離不遠的：be close to

近親：close relatives

近日：recently

⑪ 17 員 　拼音　yuán　ㄩㄢˊ

正體字	簡體字	手　寫
員	员	員

甲骨文	金　文	小　篆
（圖）	（圖）	（圖）

筆　順：員 員 員 員 員 員 員 員 員 員 員 員 員 員

🔔 周圍：surroundings

　　幅員廣大：a vast territory

🔔 工作或學習的人：people who work or learn

　　學員：student

　　員工：staff, employee

> 好員工應負責任。
> Good employees should be responsible.

⑪ 18 圓 　拼音　yuán　ㄩㄢˊ

正體字	簡體字	手　寫
圓	圆	圓

甲骨文	金　文	小　篆
		（圖）

筆　順：圓 圓 圓 圓 圓 圓 圓 圓 圓 圓 圓 圓 圓

🔔 環形，沒有稜角的形狀：a circle

　　圓桌：round table

🔔 形容完整周全：thorough

　　圓滿：satisfactory

> 這件事終於圓滿完成了。
> It was finally satisfactorily completed.

🔔 錢幣的單位詞：a unit of Taiwanese currency

　　伍拾圓：fifty dollars

⑪ 19 書　拼音　shū　ㄕㄨ

正體字	簡體字	手寫	筆順
書	书	書	書書書書書書書書書書

甲骨文	金文	小篆
	書	書

🔔 有文字或圖畫的冊子：a book

　　書本：books

🔔 文件：document

　　說明書：instructions

　　使用新產品應該先看清楚說明書。
　　Read through the instructions before using the product.

🔔 寫：to write

　　書寫：to write

⑪ 20 畫　拼音　huà　ㄏㄨㄚˋ

正體字	簡體字	手寫	筆順
畫	画	畫	畫畫畫畫畫畫畫畫畫畫

甲骨文	金文	小篆
	畫	畫

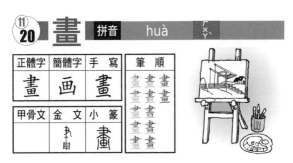

🔔 繪圖：drawing

　　畫圖：to draw a picture

　　學校在兒童節舉辦小朋友的畫圖比賽。
　　Our school held a children's drawing competition on Children's Day.

🔔 圖或圖像：picture, image

　　肖像畫：portrait

🔔 清楚、整齊：clear, neat

　　整齊畫一：neat and tidy

11/21 晝 拼音 zhòu ㄓㄡ

正體字	簡體字	手 寫
晝	昼	晝

甲骨文	金 文	小 篆

筆 順
晝 晝 晝
晝 晝
晝 晝
晝 晝

白天：day

　白晝：daylight

　晝伏夜出：hide by day and come out at night

> 貓頭鷹是晝伏夜出的動物。
> Owls hide by the day and come out at night.

11/22 夜 拼音 yè ㄧㄝ

正體字	簡體字	手 寫
夜	夜	夜

甲骨文	金 文	小 篆

筆 順
夜 夜
夜 夜
夜 夜
夜

天黑：darkness

　黑夜：dark night

從天黑到天亮之間的一段時間：the period between nightfall and sunrise

　夜以繼日：around the clock

> 我夜以繼日的趕這個案子。
> I worked around the clock to finish this project.

昏暗的：dusky

　夜色：the dim light of night

11/23 直

| | 拼音 | zhí | ㄓˊ |

正體字	簡體字	手 寫	筆 順
直	直	直	直 直 直 直 直 直 直 直 直 直

甲骨文	金 文	小 篆
		直

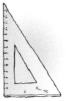

🔔 不彎曲：not curved

　直線：straight line

🔔 不邪惡，沒有私心的：not evil, unselfish

　正直：honest, upright, fair-minded

> 他是一個聰明正直的人。
> He is a smart and decent man.

🔔 縱的：vertical

　鉛直線：vertical line

11/24 真

| | 拼音 | zhēn | ㄓㄣ |

正體字	簡體字	手 寫	筆 順
真	真	真	真 真 真 真 真 真 真 真 真 真

甲骨文	金 文	小 篆
		真

🔔 純正的、不虛假的：genuine

　真心誠意：heartfelt

> 對妳的感激，我是真心誠意的。
> I am grateful to you. I mean it.

> 這幅畫是達文西的真蹟。
> This painting is a genuine picture by Leonardo de Vinci.

🔔 本性：nature

　天真：naive

🔔 姓氏：a surname

11/25 值 拼音 zhí ㄓ´

正體字	簡體字	手 寫	筆 順
值	值	值	值 值 值 值 值 值 值 值 值 值

甲骨文	金 文	小 篆
		值

Price 5300

☆ 價格：price
  價值：value
☆ 價值相稱：same value, value matches
  值得：worth
☆ 執行勤務：on duty
  值班、值勤：on duty

  這個星期日輪到我值班。
  I am on duty this Sunday.

11/26 植 拼音 zhí ㄓ´

正體字	簡體字	手 寫	筆 順
植	植	植	植 植 植 植 植 植 植 植 植 植 植 植

甲骨文	金 文	小 篆
		植

☆ 花草樹木的總稱：a general name for flowers, grass, and trees
  植物：plants
☆ 栽種、培育：to plant, grow, raise
  種植：to plant, grow

  春天適合種植花木。
  It is best to plant flowers and trees in spring.

11/27 師 拼音 Shī ㄕ

正體字	簡體字	手寫	筆順
師	师	師	師師師師師師師師師師

甲骨文	金文	小篆
	𠂤	師

🔔 軍隊：army

出師：dispatch troops to fight

🔔 教授學問、知識的人：people who teach

師傅：master, teacher

> 他是個經驗豐富的師傅。
> He is an experienced master.

🔔 具有專門技藝的人：people who have a specialized skill

廚師：cook

律師：lawyer

11/28 帥 拼音 shuài ㄕㄨㄞˋ

正體字	簡體字	手寫	筆順
帥	帅	帥	帥帥帥帥帥帥帥帥帥

甲骨文	金文	小篆
	𠂤	帥

🔔 軍隊中級別最高的指揮官：top military leaders

統帥：commander in chief

🔔 面容俊俏或舉止瀟灑、有風度：somebody who is handsome, dashing, refined

帥氣：dashing

> 你這身打扮，看起來真是帥氣！
> You are handsome in this outfit.

⑪ 29 爭 拼音 zhēng ㄓㄥ

正體字	簡體字	手 寫	筆 順
爭	争	爭	爭 爭 爭 爭 爭 爭 爭 爭 爭 爭

甲骨文	金 文	小 篆
𠂔		𤔲

🔔 奪取、互不相讓：to rob, not willing to compromise

爭奪：to fight over, vie for

🔔 辯論：to debate

爭執：to argue

爭論：to argue

> 別再爭執了，有話好好說！
> Stop arguing! Can't we talk calmly?

⑪ 30 淨 拼音 jìng ㄐㄧㄥ

正體字	簡體字	手 寫	筆 順
淨	净	淨	淨 淨 淨 淨 淨 淨 淨 淨 淨 淨 淨 淨 淨 淨

甲骨文	金 文	小 篆
		𤃕

🔔 清潔：clean

乾淨、潔淨：clean

> 乾淨的環境令人感覺舒服。
> Clean surroundings make people feel good.

🔔 純粹的、實質的：pure

淨利：net profit

*12*月
December

⑫ 1 靜 拼音 jìng ㄐㄧㄥ

正體字	簡體字	手寫
靜	静	靜

甲骨文	金文	小篆
	𩇫	靜

筆順
靜靜靜靜
靜靜靜靜
靜靜靜
靜靜靜
靜靜靜

🔔 安定不動的：stationary
　靜止：be still
🔔 沒有聲音的：silent
　安靜：silence
🔔 沉著、理智：reasonable
　冷靜：calm

請先冷靜，沒有解決不了的事情。
Calm down please. Nothing is unsolvable.

⑫ 2 掙 拼音 zhēng ㄓㄥ

正體字	簡體字	手寫
掙	挣	掙

甲骨文	金文	小篆

筆順
掙掙掙
掙掙
掙掙
掙掙
掙

🔔 用力拉扯：to pull hard
　掙脫：to struggle
　掙開：to shake off

他努力的想掙脫貧窮的生活。
He struggled to escape poverty.

🔔 爭奪：to fight for (pronounced zhèng ㄓㄥˋ)
　掙面子：to save face

 睜　拼音　zhēng　ㄓㄥ

正體字	簡體字	手 寫	筆 順
睜	睜	睜	睜睜睜 睜睜睜 睜睜睜 睜睜睜 睜睜
甲骨文	金 文	小 篆	

🔔 張開眼睛：open one's eyes

　　睜眼：open one's eyes

> 你簡直是睜眼說瞎話，毫不講理！
> You are lying. You told a barefaced lie.

 黑　拼音　hēi　ㄏㄟ

正體字	簡體字	手 寫	筆 順
黑	黑	黑	黑黑黑 黑黑黑 黑黑 黑黑 黑黑
甲骨文	金 文	小 篆	
夹	枀	㷴	

🔔 顏色：color

　　黑色：black

> 他喜歡穿黑色的衣服。
> He likes wearing black clothes.

> 你讀過《黑神駒》這本名著嗎？
> Have you read "*Black Beauty*"?

🔔 昏暗無光的：dark

　　黑暗：darkness

🔔 專門從事非法的：illegal or illicit

　　黑道：underworld, mafia

12/5 取 拼音 qǔ ㄑㄩˇ

正體字	簡體字	手寫	筆順
取	取	取	取 取 取 取 取 取 取 取

甲骨文	金文	小篆

🔔 拿東西：to get something

　　取物：to get something

🔔 得到：to obtain

　　取暖：to keep warm

　　取勝：to win

> 用不當的方法取勝，是不好的。
> It is not good to win using inappropriate means.

12/6 娶 拼音 qǔ ㄑㄩˇ

正體字	簡體字	手寫	筆順
娶	娶	娶	娶 娶 娶 娶 娶 娶 娶 娶 娶 娶 娶

甲骨文	金文	小篆

🔔 男生和女生結婚，把女生接過來的動作：
　　to marry

　　娶妻：to marry a woman

> 娶妻生子是他的生活目標。
> The goal of his life is to marry a woman and have children.

正體字	簡體字	手 寫	筆 順
零	零	零	零零零零零零零零零零零零零零零

甲骨文	金 文	小 篆
		雨令

☆ 等於數字「0」：the number "zero"

☆ 不成整數，有餘數的：not a whole number, not an integer, remainder

零頭：change left over

零錢：change

零錢不用找了，就當作小費吧！
Keep the changes as your tip.

☆ 零散的：scattered

正體字	簡體字	手 寫	筆 順
票	票	票	票票票票票票票票票票票票票票票

甲骨文	金 文	小 篆
		燹

☆ 用來作為憑證的紙張：a paper used as evidence

車票：ticket (train, bus)

選票：vote, ballot

我投他一票。
I cast one ballot for him.

☆ 紙幣：paper money

鈔票：paper money

☆ 非職業性質的演出：amateur performances

玩票：amateur

⑫9 頭 拼音 tóu ㄊㄡˊ

正體字	簡體字	手寫
頭	头	頭

甲骨文	金文	小篆
	𠆢	頭

筆順
頭頭頭頭
頭頭頭
頭頭頭
頭頭頭
頭頭頭

🔔 人或動物頸部以上的部分：head

人頭：human head

🔔 事物的開端或結束點：the beginning or ending point

從頭開始：to start all over

🔔 量詞，計算牛、羊、豬等牲畜的單位：a measure word, a unit used for cattle, sheep, and pigs

一頭牛：a cow

⑫10 腦 拼音 nǎo ㄋㄠˇ

正體字	簡體字	手寫
腦	脑	腦

甲骨文	金文	小篆

筆順
腦腦腦
腦腦腦
腦腦腦
腦腦
腦腦

🔔 掌管知覺、運動、思維、判斷、記憶等的器官：the brain

頭腦：brains

> 她頭腦很清楚，永遠知道自己要什麼。
> She has a clear mind and always knows what she wants.

🔔 人的頭部：human head

腦袋：brain, mind

12/11 惱

拼音	não	ㄋㄠˇ

正體字	簡體字	手寫	筆順
惱	恼	惱	惱 惱 惱 惱 惱 惱 惱 惱 惱 惱 惱 惱

甲骨文	金 文	小 篆

🔔 生氣、發怒：to get angry

　惱火：to get angry

🔔 煩憂、苦悶：anxiety

　煩惱：to be vexed

　苦惱：to be distressed

> 慾望是煩惱的根源。
> Desire is the root of vexations.

12/12 時

拼音	shí	ㄕˊ

正體字	簡體字	手寫	筆順
時	时	時	時 時 時 時 時 時 時 時 時 時

甲骨文	金 文	小 篆
		時

🔔 季節：season

　四時：four seasons

🔔 量詞，計算時間的單位：a measure word for time

　一小時：an hour

🔔 常常：frequently, usually

　時常：often

> 我上班時常忘了攜帶手機。
> I often forget to bring my cell phone to work.

⑫ 13 飛 | 拼音 | fēi | ㄈㄟ

正體字	簡體字	手寫	筆順
飛	飞	飛	飛飛飛飛飛飛飛飛飛飛飛飛飛飛
甲骨文	金文	小篆	
		飛	

🔔 飛翔：to fly, hover

  飛行：flying

  > 長途飛行，令我覺得很疲憊。
  > Long distance flights exhaust me.

  飛吻：to blow a kiss

🔔 速度很快的：very fast

  飛奔：run like the wind

⑫ 14 錢 | 拼音 | qián | ㄑㄧㄢˊ

正體字	簡體字	手寫	筆順
錢	钱	錢	錢錢錢錢錢錢錢錢錢錢錢錢錢錢錢錢錢錢錢錢
甲骨文	金文	小篆	
		錢	

🔔 貨幣的通稱：currency

  錢幣：coin, money

🔔 錢財：wealth

  有錢：wealthy

  金錢萬能：Money talks.

🔔 裝錢用的：something used to hold money

  錢包：wallet

  > 這是個有民俗風的錢包。
  > This wallet has a traditional feel to it.

⑫15 渴 拼音　kě　ㄎㄜˇ

正體字	簡體字	手　寫	筆　順
渴	渴	渴	渴渴渴 渴渴渴 渴渴 渴渴 渴渴

甲骨文	金　文	小　篆
愒		䁵

🔔 口乾想喝水的感覺：thirsty

　　口渴：to feel thirsty

　　解渴、止渴：to quench one's thirst

🔔 急切：eager/urgent

　　渴望：desire

　　渴求：eager

> 我渴望嘗到成功的美味。
> I am eager to taste the sweetness of success.

⑫16 喝 拼音　hē　ㄏㄜ

正體字	簡體字	手　寫	筆　順
喝	喝	喝	喝喝喝 喝喝喝 喝 喝喝 喝喝

甲骨文	金　文	小　篆
		喝

🔔 飲用液體或飲料：to drink

　　喝水：to drink water

　　喝酒：to drink wine

> 喝酒不開車。
> Do not drink and drive.

🔔 大聲喊叫：to cry loudly (pronounced hè ㄏㄜˋ)

　　喝采：to acclaim, to cheer

⑫ 17 叫 　拼音　 jiào 　ㄐㄧㄠˋ

正體字	簡體字	手　寫	筆　順
叫	叫	叫	叫 叫 叫 叫 叫

甲骨文	金　文	小　篆
		𠱠

🔔 呼喊：to cry out

　　叫喊：to yell

> 他痛得大叫。
> He yelled in pain.

🔔 動物的叫聲：sounds made by animals

　　鳥叫：chirps of birds

🔔 稱做、稱為：be called

> 你叫什麼名字？
> What is your name?

⑫ 18 吹 　拼音　 chuī 　ㄔㄨㄟ

正體字	簡體字	手　寫	筆　順
吹	吹	吹	吹　吹 吹　吹 吹 吹

甲骨文	金　文	小　篆
𠯑	𠸐	𣢍

🔔 噘嘴用力呼氣：to blow

　　吹笛子：play the flute

> 吹竹笛是我的嗜好。
> My hobby is playing the bamboo flute.

🔔 氣流順著某方向流動：flow of air

　　風吹雨打：weather-beaten

🔔 誇口、說大話：to boast, brag, talk big

　　吹牛：to boast, to brag

12 / 19 指 拼音 zhǐ ㄓˇ

正體字	簡體字	手　寫	筆　順
指	指	指	指指指 指指指 指指指 指

甲骨文	金　文	小　篆
	𢱬	𢫏

🔔 **手指**：finger
指頭：finger, toe

🔔 指示他人行動的意思：instruct someone to do something
指揮：direct, to conduct
指導：to guide, director

> 他是這齣戲的指導。
> He is the director of this play.

12 / 20 拿 拼音 ná ㄋㄚˊ

正體字	簡體字	手　寫	筆　順
拿	拿	拿	拿拿拿 拿拿拿 拿拿拿 拿拿拿 拿

甲骨文	金　文	小　篆

🔔 用手取物或持物：take or hold something with the hand
拿起：to pick up
拿出：to take out

> 我拿杯子去倒水。
> I took a cup to get some water.

🔔 捕捉犯人：to catch the prisoner/criminal
捉拿：to arrest

12/21 新 拼音 xīn ㄒㄧㄣ

正體字	簡體字	手寫
新	新	新

甲骨文	金文	小篆
𣂉	𣂉	新

筆順：新 新 新／新 新 新／新 新 新／新 新／新 新

🔔 沒有使用過的：new
新衣：new clothes

🔔 剛開始的、始出現的：just happened
新品種：new species
新聞：news

🔔 改進或使改變，而成為新的、好的：
improved or made
改過自新：start with a clean slate

12/22 親 拼音 qīn ㄑㄧㄣ

正體字	簡體字	手寫
親	亲	親

甲骨文	金文	小篆
		親

筆順：親 親 親 親／親 親 親／親 親 親／親 親 親／親 親 親

🔔 父母：parents
雙親：parents

🔔 和自己有血緣或因婚姻而建立關係的人：
people with relationships because of blood or
marriage
親人：relatives
她是我最愛的親人。
She is my dearest relative in my family.

🔔 親手：personally

12/23 財 拼音 cái ㄘㄞˊ

正體字	簡體字	手　寫	筆　順
財	財	財	財財 財財 財財 財財 財財

甲骨文	金　文	小　篆
		財

🔔 金錢或資源的總稱：money or other wealth

　財富：wealth

　財產：property

財富無法為我們帶來幸福。
Wealth can't bring us happiness.

12/24 材 拼音 cái ㄘㄞˊ

正體字	簡體字	手　寫	筆　順
材	材	材	材材 材材 材材 材材 材材

甲骨文	金　文	小　篆
		材

🔔 木料、樹幹：timber, wood

　木材：timber

🔔 原料：materials

　建材：building materials

🔔 有才能的人：capable person

　人才：talented person

他是一位人才。
He is a talented person.

⑫25 草 拼音 cǎo ㄘㄠˇ

正體字	簡體字	手 寫	筆 順
草	草	草	草 草 草 草 草 草 草 草 草 草 草 草

甲骨文	金 文	小 篆
		艸

🔔 草本植物的總稱：the general names of the herbage

　野草：weeds

　水草：water and grass

🔔 田野、荒野：field, wilderness

　草原：grassland

> 這片草原真遼闊。
> This grassland is vast.

⑫26 藍 拼音 lán ㄌㄢˊ

正體字	簡體字	手 寫	筆 順
藍	蓝	藍	藍 藍 藍 藍 藍 藍 藍 藍 藍 藍 藍 藍 藍 藍 藍 藍 藍 藍 藍

甲骨文	金 文	小 篆
		藍

🔔 像晴朗天空般的顏色：the color of the sky on a sunny day

　藍色：blue

🔔 藍色的：blue

　湛藍：azure blue

　藍天：the blue sky

> 天空一片湛藍，萬里無雲。
> The sky is clear blue and cloudless.

🔔 姓氏：a surname

12/27 雲　拼音 yún　ㄩㄣˊ

正體字	簡體字	手　寫
雲	云	雲

甲骨文	金　文	小　篆
		雲

山中河水形成的水氣：cloud
- 白雲：cloud
- 烏雲：dark cloud

烏雲密佈是下雨的徵兆。
Dark clouds are a sign of rain.

很多：many
- 雲集：come together in crowds, gather

政商雲集。
There are a lot of politicians and businessmen gathering.

12/28 電　拼音 diàn　ㄉㄧㄢˋ

正體字	簡體字	手　寫
電	电	電

甲骨文	金　文	小　篆
	電	電

閃電：lightening
用電流來發電或使用的：electrically operated
- 電燈：light
- 電視：television
- 電話：telephone

我通常在晚間收看電視新聞。
I often watch the news on TV.

⑫ 29 紅 　拼音 húng ㄏㄨㄥˊ

正體字	簡體字	手 寫	筆 順
紅	红	紅	紅 紅 紅 紅 紅 紅 紅 紅 紅

甲骨文	金 文	小 篆
		紅

🔔 像血的顏色：the color of blood
　　紅色：red

> 紅玫瑰象徵愛與熱情。
> The red rose represents love and passion.

🔔 紅色的：red
　　紅髮：red hair

🔔 受歡迎的：be popular
　　紅人：a popular person

⑫ 30 黃 　拼音 huáng ㄏㄨㄤˊ

正體字	簡體字	手 寫	筆 順
黃	黄	黃	黃 黃 黃 黃 黃 黃 黃 黃 黃 黃 黃 黃 黃

甲骨文	金 文	小 篆
黃	黃	黃

🔔 像土地的顏色：the color of earth
　　黃色：yellow

> 黃絲帶代表著期待。
> Yellow ribbons represent hope and
> expectation.

🔔 姓氏：a surname

正體字	簡體字	手　寫	筆　順
綠	绿	綠	綠綠綠 綠綠綠
甲骨文	金　文	小　篆	綠綠綠 綠綠綠 綠綠
		綠	

一種像青草、樹葉的顏色：the color of green grass or leaves
綠色：green

綠色的：green
綠葉：green leaf

形容因生氣、著急或驚嚇時的臉部表情：unhealthily pale in the face, as from sickness, fear, anger, etc.

他臉都綠了。
His face is green.

索引
Index

聯經華語 · Linking Chinese

A Character a Day:
Mastering Basic Vocabulary for Everyday Life

漢字365：每日一字

Published in April, 2014   Price: NTD 360

| Author | Committee on Chinese Learning Materials |
| Editor in Chief | Linden Lin |

Editor	Peng Li
Chinese Editor	Yan-jia Liu
English Editor	Chris Findler
Illustrators	Su-zhen Liu, Guo-jun Hong
Cover Designer	Ya-li Lai
Layout Designer	Cong-yan Lin
Audio Director	Pure Recording & Mixing

Publisher	Linking Publishing Company
Address	4F No. 180, Sec.1, Keelung Rd., Taipei, Taiwan (R.O.C.)
Tel	+886-2-8787-6242
Fax	+886-2-2756-7668
Website	www.linkingbooks.com.tw
E-mail	linking@udngroup.com

2014年4月初版   定價：新臺幣360元

有著作權 · 翻印必究

			華語教材編委會
編　　　著			
發　行　人	林　　　載　　　爵

出　版　者	聯經出版事業股份有限公司	叢書編輯	李　　　芃
地　　　址	台北市基隆路一段180號4樓	校　　對	劉　彥　珈
編輯部地址	台北市基隆路一段180號4樓		Chris Findler
叢書主編電話	(0 2) 8 7 8 7 6 2 4 2 轉 2 2 6	内文排版	林　瓊　諺
台北聯經書房	台北市新生南路三段94號	封面設計	賴　雅　莉
電　　　話	(0 2) 2 3 6 2 0 3 0 8	錄音後製	純粹錄音後製公司
台中分公司	台中市北區崇德路一段198號	繪　　圖	劉　素　珍
暨門市電話	(0 4) 2 2 3 1 2 0 2 3		洪　國　俊
台中電子信箱	e-mail：linking2@ms42.hinet.net		
郵政劃撥帳戶	第0100559-3號		
郵撥電話	(0 2) 2 3 6 2 0 3 0 8		
印　刷　者	文聯彩色製版印刷有限公司		
總　經　銷	聯合發行股份有限公司		
發　行　所	新北市新店區寶橋路235巷6弄6號2樓		
電　　　話	(0 2) 2 9 1 7 8 0 2 2		

本書如有缺頁，破損，倒裝請寄回台北聯經書房更換。　ISBN　978-957-08-4367-5 (軟精裝)
聯經網址：www.linkingbooks.com.tw
電子信箱：linking@udngroup.com

國家圖書館出版品預行編目資料

漢字365：每日一字/華語教材編輯委員會編著 .
初版 . 臺北市 . 聯經 . 2014年4月（民103年）. 224面 .
9.8×21公分（聯經華語・Linking Chinese）
ISBN　978-957-08-4367-5（軟精裝附光碟）

1.漢字

802.2　　　　　　　　　　　　　　　103003168